Changing Everything

Also by Molly McAdams

Changing Everything

A FORGIVING LIES NOVELLA

MOLLY McADAMS

wm
WILLIAM MORROW IMPULSE
An Imprint of HarperCollinsPublishers

Excerpt from *Trusting Liam* copyright © 2015 by Molly Jester.

Excerpt from *When Good Earls Go Bad* copyright © 2015 by Megan Frampton.

Excerpt from *The Wedding Band* copyright © 2015 by Lisa Connelly.

Excerpt from *Riot* copyright © 2015 by Jamie Shaw.

Excerpt from *Only In My Dreams* copyright © 2015 by Darcy Burke.

Excerpt from *Sinful Rewards 1* copyright © 2014 by Cynthia Sax.

Excerpt from *Tempt the Night* copyright © 2015 by Dixie Brown.

EPub Edition MARCH 2015 ISBN: 9780062391407
Print Edition ISBN: 9780062391414

10 9 8 7 6 5

To you, you know who you are. I will always remember you fondly as my best friend and will cherish the many fun memories with you.

Prologue
————————————————

August 30, 2013

Paisley

I FIDGETED WITH my coffee cup as I tried to find the courage to say what I'd held back for so long. Twelve years. Twelve years of waiting, hoping, and aching were about to come to an end. With a deep breath in, I looked up into the blue eyes of my best friend, Eli, and tensed my body as I began.

"This guy I met, Brett, he's—well, he's different. Like, he's a game changer for me. I look at him, and I have no doubt of that. I have no doubt that I *could* spend the rest of my life with him." I laughed uneasily and shrugged. "And I know that sounds crazy after only a few weeks, but, honestly, I knew it the first day I met him. I don't know how to explain it. It wasn't like the world stopped turning or anything, there was just a feeling I had." Swallowing past the tightness in my throat, I glanced away for a moment as I strained to hold on to the courage I'd been building up all week. "But there's this other guy, and I swear this guy owns my soul."

Eli crossed his arms and his eyebrows rose, but I didn't allow myself to decipher what his expression could mean at that moment. If I tried to understand him—like I always did—then I would quickly talk myself out of saying the words I'd been thinking for far too long.

"Eli," I whispered so low the word was almost lost in the chatter from the other people in the coffee shop. "I have been in love with you since I was thirteen years old," I confessed, and held my breath as I waited for any kind of response from him.

Nothing about him changed for a few seconds until suddenly his face lost all emotion. But it was there in his eyes, like it always was: denial, confusion, shock.

I wanted to run, but I forced myself to blurt out the rest. "I've kept quiet for twelve years, and I would've continued to if I hadn't met Brett. These last few weeks have been casual, but I know he wants it to be more. But if there is a chance of an us, then there would be absolutely no thoughts of anything else with him."

Eli just continued to stare at me like I'd blown his

mind, and my body began shaking as I silently begged him to say something—anything.

After twelve years of being his best friend, of being used by him as a shield from other women, of being tortured by his pretending touches and kisses . . . I was slowly giving up on us. I couldn't handle the heartache anymore. I couldn't stand being unknowingly rejected again and again. I couldn't continue being his favorite person in the world for an entirely different reason than he was mine. I couldn't keep waiting around for Eli Jenkins.

This was it for me.

"Eli, I need to know." I exhaled softly and tried to steady my shaking as I asked, "Is there *any* possibility of there being an us?"

Chapter One

Two months earlier . . . July 5, 2013

Paisley

"YOU LOOK LIKE someone just ran over your cat, wrapped it in Christmas paper, and delivered it to you for your birthday while saying, 'Trick or treat.'"

I blinked quickly as the bar where we spent most of our Friday nights, O'Malley's, came back into focus. I shot my friend Kristen a look, and stammered, "I don't have a ca— My birthday is in September . . . Wait, none of that made sense."

She jerked her head in the direction I'd been staring blindly at. "Exactly, and if he'd taken one look in this direction, he would've dropped that girl like she was on fire and come running over here to see what was wrong with you."

"That obvious?" Kristen nodded, and I groaned. "The only good thing about Eli being in Texas last weekend was I didn't have to watch him doing this."

Looking over to where my best friend was currently pulling close some girl he'd just met as he leaned down to kiss her, I swallowed past the lump in my throat and looked away as I tried to ignore the way it felt like I was five seconds from throwing up.

Five . . . four . . . three . . . two . . .

"Pay!"

"Oh no," I breathed, and looked at Kristen to act like I hadn't heard Eli. "If he makes me play pool with him while he makes out with another girl *again*, I will lose it!"

"He's smiling, at least he didn't see you moping—and he's walking over here. With her. Right now. He's—"

"Pay, we're gonna head out, were you ready to leave?"

I turned to look at them with a smile plastered on my face, but it was entirely possible I looked like I was grimacing. "Well . . ." I began, but the girl in Eli's arms held up her hand.

She made a sickened face as her head jerked up to look at Eli, then back at me. Long seconds passed as she looked me up and down with her lips parted in disgust. "Um . . . *ew!* I'm, like, not really into that whole threesome thing. *So* gross. Yano?"

I wanted to remind her that "you" and "know" were two separate words . . . but with the way she looked, I was surprised she knew that Eli plus her plus me equaled three and not the color burrito, so I kept that to myself.

Eli's face pinched together like he'd eaten something sour, and before he said something that would inevitably crush me even more tonight, I tried to speak his latest pick's language. "Ohmigod, like, ew, right?"

Kristen's hand flew to her mouth as beer sprayed out, and Eli's lack-of-amused expression let me know that he knew what I was doing.

At least I didn't feel like I was going to throw up anymore.

"Threesomes are so way gross," I continued, not like I'd know. But the girl nodded her head and pursed her lips.

"So, like, is she gonna watch?" she asked, and it took everything in me not to shoot Eli a look that said: *Really? This is what you want?*

"No, she's not, and there's no threesome. This is my best friend, Paisley, I drove her."

The girl laughed awkwardly and ran her hand up Eli's chest. "Well, can't she get, like, a ride home or something?"

Of course I could, and it was something that happened often when Eli decided he wanted to drive me somewhere—because chances were he was going to end up leaving with someone else, and I always offered to stick around. But I knew right then, as did Kristen, judging by her snort, that I wouldn't be getting a ride home with anyone other than Eli, and this girl had just made sure her night with Eli was over.

Eli's eyes widened and he blinked slowly before looking down at the girl. "No, she can't. I just told you, she's my best friend. She came with me, and she's going to be leaving with me . . . you won't."

"Are you serious?" she scoffed when Eli moved her arm away.

"Time to go." Eli's eyes were hard, and his voice was soft and dark. He was so pissed at me.

I cleared my throat and looked away from him. "Uh, I think I'm gonna stay with Kris—"

"Truck, Paisley."

Crap. Kristen and I exchanged a glance as I grabbed my purse and avoided looking at the livid girl still standing there. From her speech that showed how much her bleaching had lowered her IQ, I had no doubt she was still trying to figure out what all this meant.

Following Eli out to his truck, I worried my bottom lip the closer we got without him ever saying a word. Usually if a girl suggested he should leave me behind, and we left immediately after, Eli couldn't shut up about the girl's boldness. For him to not say a word only solidified the fact that he was mad about the way I'd responded to her.

I don't know what he expected from me. He chose the most ridiculous girls—and that had nothing to do with the fact that I wanted him to choose me. Okay, maybe a little, but I'm pretty sure the girl just now used the foundation color burnt orange, and had been dropped on her head way too many times as a baby.

Eli didn't need to go for the stupid, slutty girls. He was smart, had an incredible job in advertising, wore suits most of the time because of said job, and had women of all ages turning their heads to look at him.

But I knew *why* he went for them more often than not . . . because the majority of them didn't expect anything from him after that night.

We were driving out of the parking lot before he said anything. As always, his voice was calm, but his tone let me know he was anything but.

"What was that?"

"What?" I countered, and crossed my arms as I stared out the window.

"Paisley," he growled in warning.

I huffed and turned so my back was against the door and I was facing him. "Come on, Eli, she was awful— even by your standards. You know there are girls here in Yorba Linda who actually look human."

"What is that supposed to mean?"

"She had white lipstick and orange foundation. She was one bad encounter with green Jell-O powder away from being an Oompa-Loompa. Actually, you should be thanking me. If anything, I saved you from catching herpes or something."

Eli's lips tilted up in the corners, and when he spoke again, I knew his anger was slowly fading. "That doesn't mean you need to make fun of her."

You don't need to flaunt all of them in front of me either, I thought lamely. I sighed and rested the back of my head against the window. "She didn't notice."

"I did."

I stayed silent for a long time after and curled my legs up to my chest, trying to ignore the way I felt hearing his disappointment in me. Looking up when the truck stopped, I dropped my legs and cocked my head.

"Uh . . ."

He didn't say anything as he got out and rounded the front to open my door.

"Are you not taking me home?"

"Nope." Pulling me out of the truck, he grabbed on to my wrist and began towing me into his apartment.

"Eli," I complained, and tried to pull back. He just grabbed me up in his arms and started jogging—like I weighed nothing at all. "Put me down!" I demanded, but I couldn't stop laughing from the uncomfortable bouncing.

"Open." Dropping the keys on my stomach, he quickly moved his arm back to continue holding me.

I fumbled for the keys and had to steady my breathing and focus on each key as I tried to find the correct one. It's not like I hadn't opened this door thousands of times, but he was breathing heavy and holding me in his arms, and about to walk me into his apartment—and I was turning into the girl he'd been with at the bar. I wasn't sure I knew how to count to unicorn.

As soon as I had the door unlocked and opened, Eli walked us inside and kicked the door shut.

"You can put me down now," I whispered, and he snorted.

"You changed my plans for the night, Pay, so now

you have to celebrate with me." Setting me down on the kitchen counter, he turned and grabbed a box of cupcakes and pulled two out. Gently tearing the tops off both, he handed me the tops and began unwrapping the bottoms. "And now I don't have anyone to eat these with, so you're up. Get ready for a sugar coma."

My mouth had been tilting up into a smile as I'd watched him get my favorite parts of the cupcakes for me . . . but his words had just clicked, and my smile fell. Looking at the two frosted tops in my hands, I asked, "So, you'd been planning to eat these with her?"

He nodded and winked as he bit into one of the bottoms. "More or less."

"Got it." I nodded with him and bit down on my lip.

Part of me wanted to smash the frosting and cake into his face for not seeing what he was doing to me, for how much he was killing me . . . but the rest felt too sick to do anything. My arms dropped to my lap, and I set the tops onto the counter before sliding off it.

"Are you not going to eat them?"

Turning to look up at him, I swallowed roughly. "No, I don't feel that great. I'm just gonna call a cab and go home. I need to get my purse out of your truck though."

His brow furrowed. "One, when have I ever let you call a cab? Two, if you don't feel well, I'm not letting you leave. Three . . . no."

"Eli, it's not a big deal. It's not late, why don't you go back out so you can have fun instead of spending the night with me while I'm being all lame? Find another

Oompa-Loompa to bring back and share the rest of your cupcakes with, or something."

Brushing the cake off his hands, he hooked an arm around my neck and started walking out of his kitchen. "You're the only one who eats all the frosting for me, I'm not leaving you alone if you're sick—"

"Eli—"

"—and you're Oompa-Loompa enough."

My shoulder's sagged. "I am *not* orange."

"You're short, you're halfway there." With a sly grin, he pushed me toward his room. "Change, I'll go get your purse and be right back."

I sighed and stared at the closed bedroom door for a few seconds after I heard his footsteps retreat down the hall. This wasn't what I wanted. I wanted to go home and take a long bath as I tried to forget the pain of being invisible to the man I loved. Not curl up on his bed with him like we'd done hundreds of nights since we were in college. Because all that would do would make me believe I could have the life with him that I was craving.

And that just wasn't happening.

With one hard knock before the door opened, Eli poked his head in before walking all the way inside his bedroom. His lips tilted up on one side as he walked past me to change. "You always look like such a lost little girl when you're in my clothes."

Crossing my arms under my chest, I dropped my head to stare down at the floor and tried to ignore the tightening in my throat. *He's not trying to hurt you. He's not trying to hurt you* . . . My stomach clenched and my chest ached from his millionth reminder that he saw me as nothing more than his best friend.

"Hey," he crooned, and tilted my head back. "Fuck, you don't look good at all."

"Language."

Eli's expression fell. "Do you want me to get you something before we go to bed?"

I shook my head, and my lips thinned into a hard line. "I would rather go home."

His blue eyes ran over my face, the worry in them was clear. "Not happening. Get in bed."

Not giving me an option—and not like I thought I would get my way anyway—he flipped off the lights, pulled me over to his bed, and propped up all the pillows the way I liked and knew he hated. Crawling onto the bed, I waited until he was on the bed with me and sitting up against the pillows with his arm stretched out for me, before curling into his side as he pulled the comforter over us.

"You're not going to be able to fall asleep like this," I stated dully.

He turned on the TV, leaving the volume down low, and tightened his arm around me. "I'm not tired. Just feel better, Pay . . . let me know if you need anything."

I wanted to tell him medicine wouldn't help me, but that would just move into a conversation I didn't have the guts to have with him. Not when I was constantly being reminded that he didn't share my feelings.

Within three minutes, Eli's head had tilted back and

lips parted as he fell asleep. His hand flexed against my arm, and I smiled as I allowed myself this time with him. This time when I didn't have to worry about whether or not he would say something that would crush me again. Breathing in his clean scent, I let my body relax into his, and prayed for this night to never end.

"Happy birthday, Eli," I whispered, and placed my lips to his chest before falling into a peaceful sleep.

July 28, 2013

Eli

MY EYES FLEW open when I heard the front door shut. Looking to my right confirmed Carrie was still in my bed. Trying not to wake her—but moving as quickly as I could—I got out of bed and grabbed my jeans off the floor. Pulling them on as I opened my bedroom door and crept down the hall, I strained to hear anything before glancing into the living room.

Whoever it was sounded like they were in the kitchen and weren't trying to be quiet. I slowly rounded the corner, but relaxed and smiled when I saw Paisley's purse lying on the floor.

"Morning," I said as I walked past the wall blocking me from the kitchen.

Paisley jumped before a laugh bubbled up from her chest. "God, make a noise or something to warn me you're coming next time." Her brown eyes flashed down to my chest, and she quickly turned to go back to messing with whatever she'd brought over. "Don't you have a shirt you can put on?"

Stepping up behind her, I rested my chin on top of her head and picked at the pastry she'd just pulled out of the bag. "I do, but you woke me up."

"I woke you up? I'm late. And your head is heavy," she grumbled.

I put more pressure on her head and she elbowed my stomach. "What's this?" I asked, and pointed at the wrapped sandwich she'd just set down.

"There are two sausage English muffins for you."

"Do they have—"

"Extra cheese? Yes, they do."

I hugged her waist tightly. "You're the best." Grabbing one of the sandwiches, I unwrapped it and held it in front of her so she could have the first bite before taking my own. "I forgot it was Sunday," I mumbled around the food.

She laughed and started to unwrap her own sandwich. "Good thing it was my week to get food or I'd be sitting at my apartment starv— Wait. If I woke you up, why are you in jeans?"

"I could've walked out here naked."

Her body went stiff. "You don't sleep naked."

I pointed in the direction of my room with my sandwich. "Carrie's here."

"Who's Carrie?"

"The girl from the bar a few weeks ago."

"There are a lot of girls from O'Malley's when it comes to you, Eli," she countered.

"Ouch. The girl from the night of my birthday."

"Oompa-Loompa?"

"Pay," I growled in warning.

Paisley pushed against the island, trying to move me away. "Move, I need to leave."

"No, you don't."

"You have a girl in your bed who is probably as naked as you were five minutes ago. I should not be here when she wakes up."

"And you're my best friend and it's Sunday morning. This is our tradition and she's not going to stop it because I forgot what today was."

"Eli, let me go!" she hissed and jammed both her elbows into my stomach.

I bent forward as I took a step back. "Fuck, Pay!"

"Language! Let the Oompa-Loompa eat my breakfast, she'll think you did something nice for her." She took three steps away from me before I was able to grab her hand to stop her. Turning quickly, she stepped back up to me and tried to get in my face. All five feet of her. "Do you know how horrible you look when you do things like this to all these girls?" she seethed. "You're twenty-five, Eli, grow up and stop being such a whore! Stop treating every girl you meet like all she is to you is your next lay. Stop *letting* them all be your next lay! Find someone who you actually want to spend your time with and—"

"Ohmigod. Are you, like, everywhere?"

Paisley whipped her head to the side to look at Carrie,

but I couldn't take my eyes off of Pay. Where was this coming from? She'd joked about all the girls I slept with, but she'd never flipped out on me like this.

"Did I interrupt something?" Carrie gasped and shrieked, "I knew it! You *are* fucking her!"

Paisley scoffed and met my gaze. "No, he's not. That should be obvious since I'm still around and none of the other girls are."

With that, she turned and quickly left the apartment. Leaving me still standing there, staring at where she'd been long after Carrie even got dressed and left.

Chapter Two

August 3, 2013

Paisley

FIDGETING WITH THE material Kristen had shoved at me a few minutes before, I turned to look at my backside in the full-length mirror and grimaced. There was no way this thing was a dress; it was way too short. Like someone-call-TMZ-my-vagina-was-one-chair-or-car-ride-away-from-saying-hello-to-the-world short.

"I need to wear jeans with this," I grumbled.

"I'll kill you if you mess with my creation. And hurry up, it's weird that there's a party in your apartment, and you're hiding out in here."

I wasn't hiding. I was waiting for Kristen to leave so I could change. Glancing at the four-inch stilettos I was in, my grimace turned into a look of horror when I realized I looked like every girl Eli normally hooked up with. "I look like I'm trying too hard."

"No, you look like you're about to make Eli Jenkins regret that he didn't snatch you up a long time ago."

I looked through the mirror at where she was kicking her feet in the air while hanging off my bed. "Exactly. Like I'm trying too hard." Looking back down at the *shirt* that deceptively made my boobs look massive, I suppressed a sigh. "And it's all gonna be for nothing."

"You don't know that," Kristen challenged in a sing-song voice.

"Eli uses me to pick up *and* ward off women. He's not about to care if you and Jason are trying to set me up with some guy."

"I beg to differ." Her voice hadn't lost the musical lilt. When I just raised an eyebrow, she groaned and rolled over so she was lying on her stomach. "He beat the shit out of homeboy who you gave your V-card to in college."

"Eli beat him up because he posted a naked picture of me with the words 'Deflowered by Johnny G' in blood red all over our dorm, which he'd taken of me while I was sleeping."

Kristen propped herself up on her elbows and held her hands out, palms up. "If that's the way you want to see it. I choose to see it like this: Even though he deserved to get his ass beat regardless because of the picture and disgusting way that frat bragged about their conquests, that was how Eli found out you lost your virginity. Eli was jealous, and it's not like Johnny tried to hide he was the one behind it all. Therefore, Eli took his anger out on the bastard."

"Lan—"

"Don't *language* me!"

I smiled and fluffed my hair one last time before turning. "*Fine*, I'm ready . . . and your theory has to be flawed since Eli had been talking to me about the girls he'd been banging, and I hooked up with Johnny to try to get back at Eli. It didn't work, just like tonight won't work."

"We'll see."

With a deep breath, I opened my door and made it two steps before Kristen's husband, Jason, was walking toward us.

"My two favorite girls; you both look beautiful." Pulling Kristen close to his side, he grabbed me in a quick hug and glanced behind him. "I'm gonna tell him, Paisley, swear to Christ I'm going to."

"Tell who, what?"

"Eli," he sneered. "He told me about what happened last weekend when you showed up for Sunday morning."

Ah. Yeah. That . . . Thanks for the reminder. I no longer felt confident in my slutty shirt-dress. I felt like a stupid girl who had no idea what she was trying to do as I was reminded of the countless times Eli had crushed me. "Yeah." I laughed uneasily. "It was kind of awkward."

"He needs to know. He would never hurt you on purpose, and he has no idea that he's doing it now. I can't sit back and keep watching you get your heart broken over him."

"Jason, no! You promised," I begged. "You swore you wouldn't tell him how I felt."

He ground his jaw and looked behind him again to make sure no one was coming down the hall. "You can't ask us to keep watching you go through this. This has to stop, and maybe if he knows how you feel, you'll find out he feels the same."

A spark of hope ignited deep in my chest, but I was quick to put it out. "You can't know that, and, besides, you're both trying to stop it now anyway. By you trying to set me up with this Sean guy, and Kristen making me look like a streetwalker . . . I know what you're really doing. You're trying to get a reaction out of Eli."

Jason didn't respond, but his neck burned red with embarrassment. Kristen had already known I'd figured them out anyway, so she didn't look apologetic.

"You'll see that tonight won't do anything. There won't be a reaction, and you just have to be okay with that."

"Pay—"

"Jason," I hissed, and stepped closer. "It's not his fault that I fell in love with him."

Grabbing Kristen's hand, I walked down the rest of my hall and into the living room, where dozens of our friends were already hanging out.

My eyes darted across the many faces, looking for Eli's, but I didn't see him or hear his voice before Jason was behind me and turning me to the left.

"Paisley, this is Sean."

I looked up and smiled at the guy in front of me. He was taller than me—not that that was uncommon—but much shorter than Eli, and had eyes I could stare at all night. But that was it. There was no pull other than the physical attraction. And only being physically attracted to someone after having the soul-aching crave I had for Eli was a letdown.

"Sean, this is Paisley—the girl I was telling you about."

He held out a hand, and a creepy smile pulled at his lips as his eyes trailed over me. "It's great to meet you, I've heard a lot—"

"Excuse us for a minute," Eli interrupted calmly, but judging from the clipped end of his sentence—and the fact that he had just put his arm around my shoulders and pulled me away from Sean—I knew he wasn't happy.

"Eli!" Jason snarled.

"What is your problem?" I asked as he towed me through the people and down my hallway.

He didn't respond until we were in my bedroom with the door shut and locked behind us. "What the fuck are you wearing, Pay?"

I couldn't even say anything about his language. I was too excited that he'd noticed what I was wearing. My lips threatened to pull into a smile, but I somehow kept my annoyed expression. "Clothes, thanks for noticing."

Eli pointed at the little piece of fabric that liked to call itself a dress. "That does *not* count as clothes. Put something else on."

Wait. What? No . . . this is supposed to be the part where you get all possessive and tell me you've been in love with me forever and push me against the wall and make use of this little scrap of fabric. Okay, *fine,* so I'd been hoping Kristen and Jason's plan would work. Sue me. "Why?"

"Because you're in next-to-nothing and sending a message that that douche was getting loud and clear. Put some pants on at least, Christ, Paisley."

Crossing my arms over my chest, I cocked my hip and sent him a challenging glare. "Good! You know what? I'm glad he understood what this outfit was meant for." At least *somebody* got it.

Eli pointed at me. "I can see your underwear, how could he *not* understand what it was meant for?"

I looked down and straightened my body as I pulled on the fabric. Like I'd said. TMZ should've been there.

"Sorry if you were excited about this guy, but it's not about to happen, not after what I just saw."

My moment of mortification stopped abruptly, and I slowly looked up at him. "I don't like any of the women you pick up, but do you see me trying to stop you from taking them home? You can't just stop me from dating these guys whenever you don't like them, Eli! Just because you don't like the fact that *someone* appreciated the way I look doesn't give you the right to throw yourself into my life to stop me from trying to find someone."

"No, Pay . . . never," he crooned, and closed the distance between us. "But I won't watch you find someone by dressing like . . . like this. And I sure as hell won't stand back while you date someone like *him.* The second Jason went to find why you and Kristen were taking too long, that guy's hand was resting on some chick's ass, and his eyes were on another. He's a prick, I'm not letting him near you."

Wow. Really? Thanks, Jason. Biting down on my lip, I raised an eyebrow and muttered, "Sounds like someone else I know."

Eli laughed loudly. "Yeah, well, I never claimed to be a saint."

"Clearly."

Turning around, he opened up the drawer that held all my jeans, and pulled out my favorite pair. I knew what he was doing, and there was no point in arguing. He wouldn't let me out of the room until he had his way—and I really hated being in this thing anyway.

"Take off those shoes," he ordered, and held out his arm for me to steady myself on as I did. Once they were off, he bent down and held my jeans open.

"I can dress myself."

"Paisley," he warned.

Rolling my eyes, I placed my hands on the backs of his shoulders and stepped into my jeans. By the time he pulled them up over my hips, I was trying to hide a smile the size of Texas.

Swatting at his hands, I buttoned and zipped the jeans and messed with the shirt-dress so it was resting on my butt instead of over. Glancing in my mirror, I had to hand it to Eli; it looked so much better like this. Not that I would tell him.

"Now *this* is my Paisley."

My breathing halted, and I looked at him in the reflection with a wide expression.

My Paisley?

"Come on, let's get back out there."

He called me his Paisley!

Grabbing on to my wrist, he walked me out of the room and back to the living room where everyone was still going on with their night. Jason was glaring at Eli, and Kristen was giving me a look that screamed she wanted details of what had just gone down in my bedroom. After a small shake of my head, her expression fell. And the second Sean walked toward me, Eli put his arm around my waist and pulled me close to his side—and didn't let me go for the rest of the party.

Not that I minded.

Hours after the party was over, and my apartment was back to looking like my apartment again, I changed into my pajamas and washed off the makeup Kristen had also somehow talked me into. Just as I was propping all my pillows up, my phone rang, and a stupid, cheesy smile pulled at my lips.

"No, I won't call a cab for you if you went and got wasted somewhere, call one yourself. If her face is orange again, just say no. The right kind of flower can get you out of any situation your dumb mouth got you in. If it's bumpy and red, you should probably go to a hospital and get that checked, and I'll be there soon to say, 'I told you so.' "

His deep laugh filled the phone, and my body responded from that sound alone. "Appreciate all that."

"What'd you forget?"

"Remember after every formal and prom in high school, and then after almost every party in college, we'd get milkshakes and either go chill on the beach, or go back to one of our places and watch movies?"

I smiled as I sank onto my bed. "How could I forget, it was my reward for being your wingman." And some of my favorite memories of growing up with Eli; because it meant that night he was with me—not someone else.

"Best wingman ever. Never making me go to a dance with anyone other than my best friend so girls wouldn't get the wrong idea. Always being there if . . . well, just always being there."

"What's bringing up this trip down memory lane? It's been, what, three years since we did that?"

"Yep . . . too long."

My doorbell rang, and I stood quickly, my brow pinching together as I took quiet steps out of my bedroom.

"Um . . . there's—"

"Are you gonna let me in?"

My heart took off, as did my feet, and I ran down my hall to the front door. Unlocking the deadbolt, I flung open the door to find Eli standing there—phone between his ear and shoulder, two shakes in hand, and wearing an old shirt and mesh nylon shorts.

"Chocolate, peanut butter for my wingman," he said softly as he handed me one of the shakes.

I stood there smiling and staring at the cup like he'd just given me something so precious.

"So I only seem to have insomnia when my best friend isn't sleeping beside me," Eli hinted with a shameless grin.

"I have the pillows propped up just the way you hate them," I offered, still speaking into the phone.

His blue eyes darkened, and voice dropped low. "That sounds perfect."

"Did you want to come in?"

He simply nodded, and everything in me heated. But I knew what this meant for him, and I knew what he was doing. I knew Eli far too well for me not to know.

He was making up for last weekend, tomorrow was Sunday morning at *my* place, and this way he was assuring me that he would be here.

He was apologizing for tonight.

And he was letting me know I was still number one for him.

If only he knew I wanted to be number one for an entirely different reason. If only he knew that having *him* protect me from someone tonight had made my week. If only he knew that him showing up right now—like this—meant the world to me.

Stepping back, I waited until he was inside before ending the call, and closed and locked the door behind him. I followed him down the hall and into my bedroom before climbing onto my bed. Watching as he moved around my bedroom, I tried not to let him see how much I loved this. The simplest acts, but acts I wanted with him every night. Flipping off the light, turning on the TV to find a movie for us to watch, and pulling his shirt off before he slid into bed next to me.

Holding his arm out for me to curl under, he pulled me in close as he got settled up against the pillows.

"Switch."

I handed him my cup and took his from him before

taking a sip. "Chocolate, banana?" He made an affirmative noise, and once he stopped moving, I got comfortable against him and sighed. "Thanks, friend."

"Anytime, wingman."

August 5, 2013

Eli

JASON SWUNG INTO my office and slapped his hand on the door. "Lunch?"

"Uh . . . yeah. Just let me send this last thing . . . done. Where are we going?"

"Deli around the corner? I can't be gone long, I'm slammed with everyone taking their vacations."

"Sure, are the girls coming?" I asked distractedly as I loosened my tie and rolled up the sleeves of my shirt.

"Nah, you'll just have to deal with looking at my beautiful face."

I snorted and followed him down the stairs and out of the building.

"What'd you do the rest of the weekend?" he asked once we'd gotten our food and were sitting down.

I shrugged, buying myself some time as I tried to finish the bite I'd just taken. "Spent the night at Paisley's after the party on Saturday, did our Sunday morning thing, went to the gym, then just chilled at my place the rest of the day. You?"

"Of course you did," Jason mumbled.

"Of course I did what?"

"Spent the night with Paisley," he answered with a challenging look. "You're twenty-five, you don't need to be having sleepovers with your best friend when there's nothing else going on between you two. It's weird."

"Dude, you know I sleep better when Paisley is next to me."

"It's weird," he repeated.

I shrugged. "It isn't to us. She's been sleeping next to me for years, and that's how I prefer it. What's weird is sleeping without her.

Jason rolled his eyes. "Whatever, I'm not getting into that with you today, but speaking of Paisley . . . thanks for being a twat block the other night, you dick."

The change of subject caught me off guard for a second, but when I remembered the guy from Paisley's party, I huffed. "You're shitting me, right?"

"When was the last time she dated anyone . . . a year ago?"

Two. But I kept that to myself.

"And then Kristen and I try to set her up with someone, and you not only make her change, you won't let her near Sean the rest of the night."

"Okay, hold on." I sat back in my chair and swallowed more food. "That guy was a creep. He was feeling up one girl and flirting with another *at the same time* when you went to get the girls." Jason looked surprised, but I kept talking before he could. "Like I told Pay when I was making her put some goddamn clothes on—and you can let Kristen know she made her look like a hooker, by the way—I'd never try to stop Pay from dating someone as long as I thought he'd be good to her. And your pick definitely wouldn't have been good to her. I was saving her from a douche who would've wanted her for all the wrong reasons, you're welcome."

Jason sat there for a few seconds with wide eyes. "Are you serious?"

"Yeah, where'd you find him anyway?"

"I went to college with him."

"Nice," I mumbled before picking my sandwich back up. "Stop trying to set Pay up. If she meets someone, she meets someone."

"That's a little hard to do with you around," he argued.

"What the fuck is that supposed to mean?"

He avoided looking at me, keeping his eyes on his sandwich like it was the most interesting thing in the world. "It means you usually scare off anyone who tries to approach her."

"Did you not just hear me? I *want* her to find someone, I just don't want her to waste her time—"

"She's your best friend, Eli, you're never going to be okay with any of the guys. I know I've only known you a couple years, but I've heard enough stories from Kristen to know you have never let a relationship of hers last. You've found a way to end it."

My eyes narrowed and I locked my jaw as I calmed myself. "Bullshit."

"Can you name any guy she dated where you didn't have a hand in ending that relationship?"

No. "She barely dates!"

He raised an eyebrow. "Exactly."

I laughed agitatedly. "Whatever. I'm not stopping her from doing shit."

"Maybe you just don't realize it. But I know this, she's about to be twenty-five. From conversations I've heard between her and my wife, she's ready to settle down and get married. Whenever she's out somewhere and you're with her—which is always—the only time you're not scaring guys away from her is when you're too distracted by the girls you're about to take home to fuck."

"I don't scare guys away from her."

"You pull her close to your side and leave your arm around her whenever they start walking toward her!"

And? "She really wants to get married?"

Jason's face looked like he couldn't understand how I didn't know that. "Yeah."

Paisley get married? But then . . . "Damn it, I'm not ready to lose my wingman . . ."

"You're gonna lose a lot more than just your wingman," he grumbled, and I raised my eyebrows at him. "You really think the two of you are still going to have your Sunday mornings when she's married? You think you'll be sleeping in her bed, or vice versa, once she starts seriously dating someone and gets engaged?"

I didn't say anything; I just sat there with my narrowed eyes directed at him.

"No, man, you're not. Not only will her boyfriend . . . fiancé . . . husband, whatever, not be okay with that; *she'll* no longer be okay with that. Because the main guy in her life isn't going to be you anymore."

My gaze dropped to the table, but I wasn't seeing anything. There was an uneasy, hollow feeling in my chest as those words replayed in my mind. *The main guy in her life isn't going to be you. . .*

"You're not going to lose just your wingman, you're gonna lose your best friend when some other guy realizes how amazing that girl is."

Now that . . . I definitely wasn't ready for that.

August 10, 2013

Paisley

"I'LL TEXT YOU her number later," I groaned, but threw in a soft laugh at the end for his benefit.

"Where are you going again?"

"Oh my God, Eli, for the fiftieth time . . . I'm going to a bonfire with a bunch of my cousins and their friends."

"And you didn't invite me?"

I stopped walking and just stood there staring off at the ocean. "Talking to you is like talking to a child, Eli Jenkins! You've asked that in that exact same wounded voice every time I've told you what I'm doing today. And for the last time, I didn't invite you because the last time you saw my cousins you pulled a Will Ferrell . . . except it worked."

"It's not my fault your cousins were wasted and actually thought we were going streaking, and ended up getting busted by the cops."

"Well, that's not how they feel about it." I moved the phone away from my face so he wouldn't hear me laughing. When I'd composed myself again, I let out a long, annoyed sigh. "The things I do for you. I'll text you her number as soon as we get off the phone, okay?"

"You're the best, Pay!"

"I know. Have a good night, don't tell me the details."

He huffed. "See you tomorrow morning?"

"As long as she's not still in your apartment, I'll be there with breakfast."

"She'll be gone. See you then."

Ending the call, I bit down on the inside of my cheek and tried to ignore another fraction of my heart being broken off by him as I texted him my friend's number.

"You're welcome," I mumbled.

Telling myself to not think about them together, and to have a good time tonight, I blew out a hard breath and walked down the beach to meet up with everyone. I breathed in the smell of the bonfire and felt myself already relaxing—there was nothing a good bonfire couldn't make better.

"Little Paisley!"

I made a face at my cousin Michael, who was only a month older than me, but still almost a foot and a half taller. He launched himself at me, and I burst into a fit of giggles when he swung me up in his arms and turned us in really tight circles.

"I'm gonna be sick, stop!" I shrieked through my laughter, but thankfully he took it as a serious threat.

"Did you get shorter?"

My eyebrows pinched together and I tried to look behind his head. "Are you—is that—are you going bald?"

His expression deadpanned and I grinned wryly at him. "That shit's not funny."

"I thought it was."

"Yeah, whatever. Come on, I'll introduce you to everyone you don't know." We didn't take four steps before he turned me toward the cooler. "Want anything?"

"Just water for now."

He nodded and slapped a guy on the back who was reaching in there. "Brett, this is my cousin Paisley."

Brett straightened and turned, his arm already stretching out to shake mine—but the second he saw me his movements faltered, and my breath caught. *Breathe, Paisley, breathe*, I reminded myself as I took in his green eyes, wild hair, crooked smile, and splash of freckles on his face. But there was something about him that not only had me forgetting how to breathe, but also had me immediately forgetting about Eli and the numerous heartaches I'd endured because of him.

Chapter Three

August 23, 2013

Paisley

"HEY, BEAUTIFUL! JUST the girl I was hoping to see."

My steps faltered at his words, and as soon as I could manage to remove the shocked expression, a huge smile crossed my face. *Did he just call me beautiful?*

I went into Eli's strong arms easily, just like I'd done for the last twelve years. Breathing in his clean, masculine scent always made me feel like I was finally at home again. When I felt his lips graze my ear, my eyes fluttered shut and I melted into his chest.

"Thank God you're here," he whispered softly, and

my heart tripped up. "The girl at your three o'clock went home with me the other night and now thinks she has some claim on me. Mind helping me out tonight?"

And there went my heart. Dropped straight through my stomach and was left lying uselessly on the floor. Was that . . . yep! That was Eli stomping on it. Again.

When I finally got my throat to work, all that came out was a breathy "Uh . . ." that was lost in the cheering throughout the bar.

"You're the best, Pay!" His mouth brushed against my neck as he leaned back, but he pulled me between his legs where he sat on the bar stool—caging me in between him and the bar.

Like always, the ear he'd just been speaking into and the line where his mouth had dragged across my neck were on fire. Where his arm locked around my waist was burning me through my shirt, and I was having trouble breathing.

But that could have also been because I was on the verge of tears.

This wasn't the first time this had happened, not by a long shot—and I knew it wouldn't be the last. Yet every time I expected it to be different. I expected him to actually want me, for his touches to mean something. And just like every other time, I swore to myself that this would be the last time I let him use me to get his psychotic girlfriends or one-nighters to go away.

I almost laughed out loud. Who was I kidding? I would do anything for him.

Everyone in the bar erupted into cheers and yells

of displeasure, snapping me out of my pity party, and I looked up at one of the many TVs hanging throughout the bar. Eli's arm constricted around my waist, pulling me impossibly closer, and his lips were at my ear again.

"I'm exhausted. We had meetings all day today, but when I was about to leave here, Laura showed up and tried to come home with me. So I just need to stick it out until she goes first. Swear to God though, I'm about to fall asleep on the bar."

A quick glance confirmed *Laura* was shooting daggers at me and was most likely the reason Eli was pulling me close again. To anyone else, he probably looked like he was whispering anything from sweet nothings to naughty promises in my ear.

If only they knew.

I nodded my head and grabbed the mostly-full Guinness in front of me. "This yours?" I don't know why I asked, who else drank Guinness other than Eli?

"Of cour—"

"Great." Without asking, I tipped the large glass back to my lips and gulped down the thick beer until there was nothing left but remnants of foam.

Eli grabbed the empty glass and set it on the counter before turning me to face him. "Christ, Pay, what was that? You hate Guinness."

I do hate it. Like really, really hate it. Oh God, how do people enjoy that stuff? My stomach felt sick from the thick liquid, and I was still making a face as if I'd just downed a shot of tequila. Looking past his head, I contemplated how fast I could make it to the door when Eli cupped my cheeks.

"Hey, look at me. What's wrong, did you have a bad day?"

Well, I just came to the depressing realization that I've been in love with you and have waited for you for twelve years—and yet I've done nothing about it and probably will never do anything about it because I'm a wimp. And I know you don't feel the same since you're using me as a shield for the umpteenth time in our friendship. So yeah, you can say it's been a bad last few minutes.

I looked to where Laura had just been standing and scanned the immediate area when I didn't find her there. "I have to go home I forgot I have morning . . . early—I have to get up early," I stammered, and pushed against one knee caging me in. Eli just held me there tighter.

Brushing loose hair away from my face, his hands went back to cupping my cheeks and forced me to look at him again. His blue eyes were wide with worry and I almost forgot what I'd been attempting to do when I saw them. I loved his eyes, I could get lost in them. Against his tan skin and dirty-blond hair, they looked like dark oceans with bolts of lightning going through them.

I started to lean into his touch, but then remembered why he was touching me. When it was just us there were hugs, arms slung around shoulders, and the nights we curled up with each other in one of our beds, but nothing more. When I was acting as his way out—it was everything I'd always craved from him. My few moments of deluding myself into thinking his touches meant something . . . my few moments of pretending.

And this was the last time I would have those moments.

My vision went blurry and I blinked rapidly against the stupid traitor tears that were threatening to spill down my cheeks.

"Paisley, you're crying?" he whispered harshly, and I felt his body go still against mine. "Tell me who they are, and what they did. Now."

The *who* was making me quickly lose my will to walk away, and the *what* was not helping by going all hero on me and holding me closer. I pushed against his chest and he responded by sliding one of his hands from my cheek to the back of my neck, bringing my face close enough that our foreheads and noses were touching.

A quick rush of air left my body and I stopped breathing for tortured moments as I realized this was the closest our lips had ever been. *He doesn't want you, Paisley. He doesn't want you.* Closing my eyes, I tried pushing against his chest again.

"Stop trying to leave," he gritted.

"You can stop touching me, your fuck buddy already left."

Eli jerked back and stared at me with open shock. Using the shock to my advantage, I pushed against his strong leg and had made it two steps away from him when he caught my arm and swung me back to him.

"Pay—"

"Let me go!"

The bar was loud enough that only a couple of our friends who had been sitting near him had heard me. But in that moment, it wouldn't have mattered if an entire city heard me yell that at him, or no one at all. I wanted to take it back. The hurt that tore through those blue eyes I loved so much caused an ache to rip through my chest, worse than the one I'd already been battling.

Instinct told me to ask him to forgive me . . . I couldn't stand the thought of him being mad at me or hurting because of something I'd done. But survival kicked in and took forefront. Because of my pathetic excuse for a backbone, he had been unknowingly hurting me since we were thirteen years old, and I couldn't take it anymore.

I needed to stop waiting around for him to fall in love with me too.

I needed to stop letting him have this control over me.

I needed to start living for me. Not for Eli Jenkins.

Wrenching my arm free from his grasp, I turned and fled from the bar. I'd just opened the door to my car when Eli's hand slapped down on the glass and slammed it shut.

"What was that, Paisley?" Before I could respond, he was talking again. "You know I don't give a shit if Laura was still there or not. If you're upset and about to start crying—you're all that matters. You're my best friend, if something's going on with you, then you have my full attention. I'd already completely forgotten about her by the time you picked up my beer."

I hated and loved that Eli wasn't the kind of guy to

yell. He'd always had a calmness about him, even in the most stressful of situations. To see him go off meant that whatever was wrong was wrong in an epic sort of way. But that didn't mean he didn't get mad. And I'd been around him long enough to pick out his emotions. It was all in his eyes and the deepness of his voice—and right now, Eli was hurt and pissed off. Knowing that, and seeing his calm exterior, was worse than just having him yell at me.

"Now I don't know why the fuck you just went off on me, but tell me right now what happened to put you in the mood you're in."

"Language," I chastised softly.

Placing his closed fist under my chin, he tilted my head back until I was looking in those hypnotic eyes again. "Paisley, you don't cry for anything. Tell me who hurt you."

You. It's always been you. Tears continued to fill my eyes as I opened my car door again.

A broken exhale left him when I stepped away and climbed into my car. "Why won't you tell me? You tell me everything. When did that change?"

When I realized I've been— And that's when it hit me. Eli wasn't hurting me. I'd been hurting myself by waiting for something I knew would never happen. I'd been hurting myself by allowing him to put us in this position.

Looking over at my best friend, and the man who had held my heart for twelve years, I wiped away tears and answered simply, "Tonight."

August 30, 2013

Eli

I HUNG UP and threw the phone against the recliner before falling onto my sofa. What the hell was happening? Paisley and I usually didn't go more than a day without talking, and that was if we were busy. It'd been a week since the night at O'Malley's and she hadn't returned any of my calls or texts. If it hadn't been for Jason saying she was with Kristen last night, I would have already filed a missing persons report for her.

Raking my hands through my hair, I held them there as I thought back to that night. I didn't even know how to explain what had happened with her. One second we're watching the game and I'm trying not to pass out from exhaustion, the next she's downing my Guinness, trying her hardest not to cry, and yelling and cussing at me.

There were a few things wrong with that picture. One, Paisley hates Guinness with a passion, and thinks German beer should be the only beer consumed. Two, I've seen her cry two times in all the years that I've known her and remembered them perfectly. When her grandpa passed, and when Johnny Gallo tried to ruin her publicly after she gave him something I wished she'd saved for someone who treated her like she was his world. Three, she has only yelled at me once and that was two days after she got her first car. We had covered her car in Post-it notes, but only after we'd finished Saran-wrapping the entire thing. And four, I have never once, in the twelve years of knowing her, heard my Paisley cuss. Ever.

I was planning another trip to her apartment when my phone went off with her ringtone, and I launched across the space from the couch to the recliner.

"Pay?" I answered, and exhaled a heavy sigh of relief when I heard her voice come through.

"Hey, Eli."

"How've you been, are you okay? Goddamn, Paisley, I don't even understand what happened last weekend."

"Language," she whispered, and a large smile crossed my face. "Do you think—uh, do you think we could talk?"

I was already going for my keys on the counter. "Of course, I'm on my way to your place."

"No!"

Jerking to a halt, I paused for a few seconds before rolling my eyes and grabbing my keys. "I'm coming to see you."

"Can you meet me at Grind?"

"You haven't answered my calls in almost a week, and you want to talk about last weekend in a coffee shop? Are you serious?"

She sighed, and when she finally answered me, her soft voice was determined. "Yes."

"All right, when?"

"I'm already here."

And I was already running out my door. "I'll be there in fifteen."

I made it in nine.

I was trying to remain calm, but everything about this last week and her phone call had me on edge. Something had happened to her, and I needed to know what it was. I found her immediately at the table we normally sat at, and tried not to look like I was stalking over to her. She didn't smile, and didn't stand to meet me like she normally did, but I needed to reassure myself my Paisley was still here and okay.

Pulling her out of the chair, I wrapped my arms around her tiny shoulders and held her close—my body relaxed when I felt her arms go around my waist.

"What happened?"

She shrugged and pulled away to sit back down, and a frown tugged at my lips even as she tried to send me a reassuring smile. "I was just being dramatic. Nothing new there."

Bullshit. "I'm going to get a coffee, how long have you been here?"

"About an hour."

"Which means this is gone," I assumed, and grabbed the empty cup. "I'll get you another."

After getting a black coffee for myself and another mocha for Paisley, I went back to the table and tried not to ask why she looked nervous as shit. Her brown eyes flickered up to mine and I felt my forehead pinch together. Was she wearing makeup? *Since when does Pay wear makeup?*

"So, uh, how's work?"

The cup stopped halfway to my lips and stayed there before I placed it roughly back on the table. A week after the weirdest fucking night of our friendship and *that's* what I get?

"Okay, what the hell is going on? I haven't seen you in a week. We never have these awkward silences. You never have to ask, '*Uh*, how's work?' And you're wearing makeup, for Christ's sake."

Her eyes brightened, and her full lips went up into a soft smile. "You noticed I'm wearing makeup?"

"Are you fucking kidding me? That's what you're going to go with out of all that?" When her cheeks darkened and her mouth formed a tight line, I sighed. "I'm a guy, but I still know what makeup is. I had to spend years trying to get Candice and Rachel not to wear that shit, so yeah, I noticed that you're wearing it."

"Langu—"

I leaned closer until I was right in front of her face and spoke low. "Language is about to get a whole lot worse if you don't clue me in on whatever's happening with you."

"I met someone," she blurted out, and I rocked back in my seat.

"What?"

"Um, I, uh—I met someone. A guy."

"No, I got what you meant. When did this happen and do I know him?"

Her eyes were glued to her cup, but I wanted her to look at me so I could understand what exactly this guy had done to her. If he'd hurt her I was going to kill him.

"A few weeks ago, and, no, you don't know him. We've gone out a lot since I met him . . ." She continued talking, but I didn't hear anything else.

She'd met this guy weeks ago and hadn't told me? And this entire week when I'd been trying to get ahold of her, she'd probably been on dates with him? Fuck. That. I didn't care who this prick thought he was. Paisley was my closest friend; I wasn't about to lose her to this guy. Especially if it meant her turning into the Paisley I'd seen the last two times we'd been together.

"Eli." Her shaky tone finally broke through my inner brooding, and I looked up at her. "I need to tell you something—and I don't want you to respond until the end when I ask you a question. Okay?"

He hurt her. I knew it. That's it; he was dead.

"Eli?"

"Yeah, okay," I growled.

Paisley's dark eyes turned sad and she shook her head. "I don't know what you're mad about, but we don't have to do this right now, we can do it later."

When she started to stand, I grabbed her hand and held her there. "No, I want to do this now, but I need to know if he hurt you, Pay. It's killing me thinking of everything this guy might have done to you."

"Of course he didn't!"

Relief surged through my body until I realized that there was still something else making her act like this. Trying to keep my tone neutral, I urged her to tell me. "Okay, I promise I'll stay quiet until your question."

Her eyes immediately fell back to her coffee cup as she took measured breaths in and out—and just when I was about to beg her to talk to me, she looked back up.

"This guy I met, Brett, he's—well, he's different. Like,

he's a game changer for me. I look at him, and I have no doubt of that. I have no doubt that I *could* spend the rest of my life with him."

Oh shit. It was like Jason said. I really was going to lose my Paisley.

"And I know that sounds crazy after only a few weeks, but, honestly, I knew it the first day I met him. I don't know how to explain it. It wasn't like the world stopped turning or anything, there was just a feeling I had." She swallowed roughly and looked away for a second. "But there's this other guy, and I swear this guy owns my soul."

There was another guy? And she hadn't said anything? We'd always told each other everything. Seriously, when the hell did all this change?

"Eli," she whispered, her voice nearly inaudible. "I have been in love with you since I was thirteen years old."

Paisley dated people about as often as the Olympics came around, and I spent nearly every day with her. How could I not have known about all these— Her declaration finally hit me, and I schooled my features before I could give away my shock.

What. The. Hell did she just say? She what? No—no way. She was my best friend. Nothing more. My mind raced as she took controlled breaths and kept up her fucked-up confession.

"I've kept quiet for twelve years, and I would've continued to if I hadn't met Brett. These last few weeks have been casual, but I know he wants it to be more. But if there is a chance of an us, then there would be absolutely no thoughts of anything else with him."

This couldn't be happening to us. She was my best friend. My wingman. She was the only girl I could stand to be around for any period of time other than my sisters, Candice and Rachel. And even those two were pushing it.

"Eli, I need to know." She exhaled slowly and waited until she held my stare. "Is there *any* possibility of there being an us?"

I sat there frozen as I replayed everything she'd just said over and over. Waiting, hoping for her to take it all back. As the minutes ticked by, her anxious posture slowly hunched in on itself, and I watched as the hopefulness left her eyes.

Not a joke. This was real.

As the confusion washed through me, my head began shaking back and forth. "You're my best friend, Paisley," I nearly whispered. "You've always just been my best friend."

A heavy breath left her when she grasped there was nothing else I would be adding, and for the second time in a week—and the fourth time in a dozen years—I watched Paisley bite down on her bottom lip as her eyes filled with tears.

"Pay . . ." I started reaching across the table, but stopped short. How was I supposed to touch her? How was I supposed to comfort her? How was I supposed to do anything now that I knew how she felt?

She blinked back the tears and it hit me. The bar—her tears. Like I'd done countless times, I'd been using her to make someone else realize I wasn't interested. I had been touching her, brushing kisses against her neck—oh

God. They meant nothing to me . . . but they'd meant something to her.

My head dropped into my hands and my elbows hit the table. If Paisley was in love with me, that changed everything . . . in the worst way possible.

"At the bar." My voice came out rough, and I tried to clear my throat. "I was the reason you were upset last weekend." I took her silence as confirmation, and even through my fear of losing my best friend, I hated myself in that moment. "I'm so sorry, Pay."

"Don't be, it's not your fault—I mean, it's not like you had any idea." She tried to laugh, but it sounded wrong.

All of this was wrong.

"I have to go," she choked out minutes later, and rushed out of the coffee shop.

I was out of my chair and running outside as soon as I heard the door shut. "Paisley," I called after her, never stopping until I had ahold of her arm and was pulling her close into my chest.

Her body shook beneath my arms, and her head stayed bent as I whispered, "I'm sorry" over and over again. Tilting her head back, I brushed at her wet cheeks. "Pay, please don't cry . . . it's killing me to know that I'm the reason behind these tears."

Paisley's eyes closed as more tears fell from them, and her jaw trembled as she clenched it tight. When she tried lowering her head again, and I wouldn't allow the movement, her eyes opened—and they were pleading with me.

What? I wasn't sure. I was just terrified that she was somehow letting me know that I was about to lose her.

That this was my only chance, and I knew it was a chance I couldn't take. I loved her, but not the way she wanted me to. I couldn't give her what she was asking for.

Kissing the top of her head, I left my lips there and prayed I wouldn't lose my best friend as I whispered, "I'm sorry I can't be what you need."

A strangled cry burst from her chest, and when she tried again, I let her leave my arms to get in her car. As I stood in the parking lot watching her drive away, I knew I'd just lost the only girl who'd ever meant anything to me.

Chapter Four

September 1, 2013

Paisley

"I DON'T KNOW why it hurt so bad to hear him say those words—it's not like I didn't know that's how he felt. It's not like it'd been some big question of whether or not he might love me too . . . I guess I'd just kept letting myself believe that when he found out, he'd maybe see things differently, or something, I don't know." Looking over at Jason, I forced out something that vaguely resembled a laugh. "I blame you for that last part."

Jason and Kristen both sat there sharing twin looks of

pity, and I hated it. All their expressions were doing was making the ache in my soul grow.

Eli wasn't in love with me.

I'm sorry I can't be what you need.

My lips thinned into a tight line, and tears filled my eyes as his words played over and over again in my head. They'd sounded tortured coming from him, and they were torturing me still two days later.

"Paisley," Kristen crooned.

"I'm fine," I lied, and tilted my head back as I blinked away the tears.

I almost never cried, but Eli Jenkins was bringing the tears out a lot lately. I didn't want them. I didn't want *this*. I didn't want to feel like nothing was right in the world. I didn't want to be hiding out at Kristen and Jason's on a Sunday morning because I was worried Eli would show up at my house and try to act like nothing had changed between us—while at the same time terrified he wouldn't show up at all. I didn't want to have a shattered soul while simultaneously having my chest tighten in anticipation at the thought of seeing Brett later. I just wanted to go back to how everything had been.

I'd spent half of my life silently loving Eli Jenkins. And up until a few weeks ago, I would have told you with one hundred percent certainty that I would have continued loving only him for the rest of my life even if he never found out—as pathetic as that sounds. I never expected to find someone who would have me reconsidering that future, and I definitely never expected to find someone who would have me falling *that* hard *that* fast.

There was no way to prepare for Brett and the impact he'd already had on my life, just like there was no way for me to prepare to lose everything I'd had with Eli. He was still my best friend, and, sure, I could have gone on with our friendship . . . but even Eli had stopped calling. He hadn't tried to contact me once since I'd driven away from Grind on Friday morning, and Jason said he hadn't shown up to work that day.

"I should have never told him . . . I should have just started the relationship with Brett."

"No. No, you shouldn't have. Because what if this thing with Brett continues? You said he's different, and I don't doubt it since it finally made you tell Eli your feelings. But what if somewhere down the road you two got married, and you're sitting there wondering what would've happened if you had just told Eli how you felt? What if you'd gotten so deep in your relationship with Brett only to find out that Eli felt the same, and then you had to choose between two men you *loved*?"

My stomach churned, and I wished I hadn't drunk that coffee. "But in telling him all that, I just pushed him away. Not only did I force him to confirm that nothing will ever happen between us, I've lost my best friend."

"That's not true," Kristen said sadly at the same time Jason assured me, "No, you haven't."

"I think it was a lot of information at once," Jason continued. "I think you probably blew his mind, and I think he needs time to think about it. You've had twelve years of falling in love with him, and he just found out forty-eight hours ago at the same time of finding out about Brett. Give him time to come around; but you haven't lost him, trust me. That guy is terrified of losing you."

My forehead pinched together. "How do you know that?"

Kristen turned to look at Jason. "Yeah. How do you know that?"

Jason rubbed at the back of his neck before slamming his hand down on the arm of the chair he was sitting in. "I kinda talked to him about you a few weeks ago. It was the Monday after that party at your apartment when we tried to set you up with Sean."

"Jason! You promised!"

He put his hands in the air, and looked around like I was missing something obvious. "I know I did, and I kept my promise. I don't know why you look so freaked out, Pay, it's a moot point now. He already knows you love him." Kristen smacked him and he looked at her. "What?"

"What did you tell him?"

"We were talking about Sean. He was mad that I'd tried to set you up with him and told me to stop trying to set you up with anyone. Said if you found someone, then you found someone—I told him that was hard to do with him around."

My eyes widened and my stomach dropped.

"We kind of argued over the fact that he makes sure guys don't approach you, and that he's always had a hand in ending whatever relationships you've had before. I told him I knew you were ready to get married and all that, and it kind of stunned him. He said he wasn't ready to lose his wingman."

I was about to cry again. I swallowed past the tightness in my throat and tried to ignore the stinging in my eyes as I waited for him to finish.

"I . . ." Jason paused, and eyed me warily before blowing out a hard rush of air. "I told him he wasn't just going to lose his wingman. I more or less told him that your nights of sleeping over with each other, and Sunday mornings, wouldn't be happening if you started seriously dating and got married. Then I might have told him he'd be losing his best friend."

Jason was still as he waited for our reactions, but I wanted to know Eli's. "What'd he say?"

"You know him better than anyone, you know he doesn't ever raise his voice. I could tell he was pissed that I was telling him how he'd been getting in the way. But once I told him he'd be losing his best friend, he couldn't even respond. He just looked sick. Didn't finish his sandwich, and didn't talk to me as we walked back to work. When I walked into his office again later that day, he still had that sick-fearful look about him."

I'm sorry I can't be what you need.

I now knew why he'd sounded so tortured when he'd said those words. He'd known he was losing his best friend.

I was right.

I'd just changed everything.

September 6, 2013

Eli

I WENT THROUGH the motions of putting on my tie, but I didn't even remember getting dressed this morning. I didn't remember much about this entire last week since Paisley had dropped that bomb on me. I went to work, ate, and slept . . . but when I'd think back on all of it . . . I didn't remember any of it.

My cell rang from where it sat on the nightstand behind me, but it wasn't Paisley's ringtone, so I let it go on until the voice mail picked up.

A week since she'd thrown my world on its side, and a week since I'd spoken to her. Everything about that was wrong, but I didn't know what to say to her—I doubted she even wanted to hear from me. I couldn't give her what she wanted from me. I hated myself for not seeing it years before so I wouldn't have continued to give her hope. I'd made my Paisley cry. Twice.

My phone rang again, but I just walked into the bathroom to brush my teeth. I didn't want to talk to anyone unless it was her. But she had Brett now . . . and I was the last person she would want to talk to about anything. Not after getting the courage to tell me what she had, only for me to let her down.

I glared over at my cell when it started up for the fourth time as I walked back out of the bathroom. Moving over to the nightstand, I looked at the screen and tapped the green button.

"Hey, Mom," I answered.

"Eli! Oh my God, Eli!"

Everything in my body jolted as her screams came through the phone. "Mom! What happened?"

"Your dad—hospital—you need—please!" she choked out between sobs.

"Mom, try to calm down and tell me what happened." Turning around, I ran through my apartment and grabbed my keys and wallet before running out the door and to my truck as she tried to tell me about Dad.

"His car exploded at the house. I was out of the city having breakfast with my sister! He—he's at the hospital, you need to be there for him! There's so much traffic, and I can't get there!" she screamed.

"Pull over until you can calm down, I'm already on my way."

"No, I need to be there!"

"Mom!" I barked, and waited for her hysteria to calm. "Take deep breaths, he's going to be okay. But you need to be okay too, so try to stay calm so you can get yourself there, all right?"

She whimpered and sniffled, but didn't respond otherwise.

"What do you mean exploded?"

"Just . . . just exploded. Blew up. In the driveway."

I blinked slowly. *Exploded? That shit happens in movies.* "Was he in it?"

"Walking toward it."

"Thank God," I whispered, but my mind wouldn't shut off. Seriously. That's movie shit. "All right, I'm on my way, just try to stay calm. I'll call you when I see him."

Ending the call, I drove as fast as Friday morning traffic would allow me to the hospital, and was quickly taken back to where my dad was. Fear flooded my veins and weakened my knees the closer we got to his room. I didn't know what to expect, I didn't know if he was in a coma, I just didn't know anything.

"What the hell happened?" I asked, my tone coated in relief when I saw him sitting up in the hospital bed.

"You're asking the wrong person. Is your mom okay?"

I shot him a look and sighed as I sat in the chair next to the bed. "Not even close, but she's on her way. You don't look anything like what I was afraid I'd find."

He laughed shakily. "Just some scratches and a bump on my head from where I hit the walkway. I mainly can't stop shaking and my ears are still ringing."

"Christ . . . you scared me, old man." I squeezed his outstretched hand and called Mom.

"Eli?" she answered frantically.

"He's fine. I'm sitting with him now. He's just a little shaken up."

She breathed a deep sigh of relief. "Oh, thank God!"

"Yeah."

"Tell him I love him and I'm on my way."

I looked up at my dad to see him smiling, and I knew he could hear her. "Will do, see you soon." Once I ended the call, I sat back again and rubbed my hands over my face. "She said you were walking out to your car?"

Dad blinked quickly. "The alarm went off on my car . . . I figured someone hit it with the newspaper or something. I tried turning it off with the key fob inside the house, and when it didn't stop, I walked outside. I was about"—he thought for a second—"halfway down the walkway to my car when it just blew up. I have no idea what happened, and I was never knocked unconscious, but I was out of it. Everything was so loud and just shaky. I still—I still can't believe that just happened. It doesn't feel like real life."

"I was thinking that," I said gruffly. "Sounds like something you see in movies."

There was a knock on the door, and two police officers walked in. "Mr. Jenkins, I'm sorry, but we had a few more questions."

I patted my dad's arm and stood. "I'm gonna go make a call."

Walking out of the room, I fell back against the wall and dropped down to the floor, letting out a shaky breath as I ran my hands through my hair. He was alive, he was fine . . . but there had been so much adrenaline pumping through my body that was now quickly fading, that I felt like I was about to crash.

And I needed Paisley.

Grabbing my phone out of my pocket, I pulled up her number and stared at it for long minutes. Just as I started to press down, I heard my name being called. Looking to my left, I saw my mom jogging down the halls and stood to meet her. She had makeup streaming down her face, and her body shook as she cried against my chest.

"Is he okay?"

"Yeah, there are officers in there talking to him." Shoving my phone back in my pocket, I turned her toward the room. "Come on, let's go in there."

I JERKED AWAKE when I heard a scream early the next morning. It was still pitch black in the room and outside the window, and it took me a second to realize where I was. It wasn't until I heard my mom and dad yelling loudly that I remembered I'd stayed at their house in case Dad needed anything. They didn't know why his car had blown up, but that shit didn't just happen out of nowhere, so I'd also wanted to be here in case anything like it happened again.

Scrambling off the bed and out of my old bedroom, I ran toward their room and nearly broke the door off the hinges when I didn't twist the knob enough and threw all my weight into it.

"What's happening?" I yelled as soon as I was in.

I looked wildly around their room as they both ran in and out of their closet. My mom was crying as she packed a suitcase, my dad was trying to calm someone down on the phone.

"What is going on?" I asked again, and my dad turned to look at me, his face filled with the terror I'd felt yesterday morning as I'd driven to the hospital.

"Rachel," he whispered to me, and shook his head, trying to convey that whatever had happened to my sister . . . it wasn't good.

Chapter Five

September 7, 2013

Eli

IT FELT LIKE I was in a daze, like none of this could possibly be real—but somehow it was. I sat in the waiting room with my parents and younger sister Candice as I waited for the time when I could go into Rachel's room again. Candice clutched at my arm as her body shook steadily, even through her sleep, and my mom cried quietly against my dad's shoulder as they whispered back and forth to each other.

Rachel and Candice were three and a half years

younger than me, and both were living in Austin attending the University of Texas there. While only Candice was blood, I'd never considered Rachel anything other than my sister. I'd just been with them a little over two months ago when I'd had a business trip here . . . and now Rachel was hooked up to a bunch of machines in a hospital room because of a stalker. The same man had apparently had people following all the members of my family, and had been behind my dad's car blowing up.

Rachel was alive and would live a normal life, and she was whole, but she in no way would be okay. Not only had she been stalked and tortured by a psychopath, she'd also found out while being rescued that her fiancé was an undercover cop. I couldn't imagine that conversation was going over well between them in her room, and I hated knowing that my sister was completely broken.

Removing Candice from my arm, I stood and walked to the other side of the waiting room to get away from them as I tried not to break down. Running my hands down my face, I let out a shuddering breath and tried to make sense of all this, but there was no way to. It still didn't feel real. I just had to be thankful they'd been trying to send a message with my dad, and not trying to kill him; and thankful for Rachel's fiancé, Kash. If it weren't for him and the other detectives, they wouldn't have found her in time.

My throat tightened at the thought of losing my sister, and like I had so many times over the past twenty-four hours, all I could think was that I needed Paisley there with me.

Pulling my phone out of my pocket, I walked out of the waiting room and down a little vacant hall. After going through the contacts, I stared at Paisley's name for a long time—just like I'd done yesterday—before finally pressing down on it.

It rang and rang until her voice mail picked up, and my head fell back to the wall when her voice filled the phone. I rubbed at the ache in my chest as I wished once again for all of this to be some fucked-up nightmare.

"Hey, Pay, happy birthday," I choked out, and cleared my throat. "I wish I could get a box of cupcakes and split them in half with you, but I'm in Texas. Some bad stuff happened to Rachel—and well . . . I'm just in Texas. So go get some cupcakes and eat the tops for me, sound good?"

I ground my jaw as I tried to figure out how to end it. *I miss you? This is killing me? I'm sorry for not being the guy need?*

Instead, I just stuttered, "Okay, yeah . . . see—uh . . . see you."

Walking back into the waiting room, I saw Kash was out of Rachel's room and sitting next to his work partner, and went over to introduce myself. I didn't like that my sister had gotten engaged without me ever meeting the guy, and I really didn't like that he'd been keeping the fact that he was an undercover cop from her, but I knew for Rachel's sake I needed to try to be nice. I cleared my throat when I stepped up to him, and when he looked up at me, I had to clear it again to make sure I'd be okay to speak after the message I'd just left.

"Eli Jenkins," I said as I offered my hand. "Thank you for saving her. She's always been like a sister." Kash didn't respond. "You're her fiancé, right?"

Pain covered his face, but he still didn't respond.

Dropping my hand, I took a step back. "I'm sure it's been a long day for you. We can talk later. I just wanted to say thank you."

"You don't need to thank me. I would do anything for her." He licked his lips and his eyes darted to her door. "Watch out for her, okay?"

For some reason, I knew he didn't mean right now. And while I didn't know what had just happened in that room, I knew it hadn't been good. Nodding, I walked quickly into Rachel's room to see her straining to keep her cries silent.

"Are you hurting?" I asked as I went to the chair near her bed.

She nodded before shaking her head. "I don't need pain medicine . . . I need the other half of my soul back."

I shakily sat in the chair and grabbed her hand. She tightened both hands around mine as I sat there staring at nothing.

My soul.

The ache in my chest and body somehow grew, and I knew—I knew then what I'd lost.

I hadn't just lost my wingman and best friend . . . I'd lost the only girl who could touch my soul.

September 7, 2013

Paisley

RELAXING INTO BRETT'S side as we walked out of the theater, I smiled up at him as he talked about the movie we'd just seen. I could listen to him talk all day about anything. His green eyes and full lips were always extremely expressive—the British accent was just the cherry on top.

He'd moved to the United States to go to college, and had never left—now staying here on a worker's visa. Not even a foot taller than me, with lean muscles compared to Eli's bulky build, and a little bit of a hipster edge to the way he dressed—he was Eli's complete opposite. And I thanked God that not one thing about Brett reminded me of him.

"So . . ."

I raised an eyebrow and giggled against his lips when he stole a kiss. "So?"

"What next, birthday girl?"

"Oh, so you didn't have this whole day planned?" I teased.

"I did." I made a face and rolled my eyes. "I do!" he reiterated on a laugh. "But if there was something *you* wanted to do first, then I want to make that happen. My plans for you can wait."

"Really?" I skipped a step in front of him and turned so I was in his arms and walking backward. "And what do your plans include?"

"Your apartment."

"Mine?"

He nodded. "And us."

"Generally a good thing not to be alone on my birthday."

Brett smiled and pressed his lips softly against mine. "And something else I can't tell you about yet."

"Seriously?" I asked when I pulled away.

"Yes, seriously. I can't give away all my secrets yet."

I narrowed my eyes and he did the same. "Fine! Fine, take me to my apartment. I want to see what you have planned for us, and there's really nothing else I want to do today."

He smiled and turned to pull me toward the parking lot.

The entire way back I tried to guess what it was, or what we might be doing. Some of my guesses earned me an eye roll, others loud laughs, and the rest heated stares that seemed to change the air between us in his car. But apparently, I was still way off.

"Yes, Paisley, clothes are staying on," he repeated again as I pushed my key into the lock. "But keep bringing some of that up, and I'll have to reconsider."

I sent him a teasing grin as I opened the door. I'd known whatever he wanted to do here had nothing to do with our clothes since we'd both talked about *trying* to go slow with our relationship. But the way his green eyes darkened when I'd mention it was quickly becoming one of my favorite things, and it was hard not to keep bringing it up to see that reaction out of him.

"Happy birthday!"

I screamed and jumped back into Brett's arms when the shouts from my friends nearly gave me a heart attack—and almost made me pee myself if I'm being honest.

He wrapped an arm around my waist and pushed me forward when I hadn't moved. Bending down so his lips were next to my ear, he whispered, "Happy birthday, Paisley."

Goose bumps covered my arms from the way his low voice curled around my name, and I looked up to kiss his jaw before stepping away into the waiting arms of my friends.

I was hugged, kissed on the cheek, and picked up dozens of times. But my eyes had never stopped moving—had never stopped looking for a tall guy built like a god, with short blond hair and perfect blue eyes. Even as I looked for him, I somehow knew he wouldn't be there, though. Not just because we hadn't talked in over a week, but I was sure my body would know when he was close again.

Looking over to Kristen and Jason in silent question as Brett pulled me into his arms again, both shook their heads faintly, and I nodded mine in acknowledgment.

"Surprise?" Brett offered.

I pushed on his stomach before wrapping my arms around his waist. "I guessed this."

"Well, of course you did. But it's not like I could just tell you. That would have ruined the best reaction I've ever seen."

"Oh God, I don't even want to know what I looked like."

"Adorable."

"Charmer?"

His lips tilted up in the most perfect crooked smile. "Absolutely."

"Thank you for this."

He jerked his head toward my living room. "Come on, let's enjoy your day, shall we?"

"HE HASN'T EVEN called you?" Kristen asked hours later. "It's your birthday. I just don't see him being like this," she mumbled mostly to herself.

Everyone except Brett, Kristen, and Jason had just left; and before I could question them about the obvious missing guest once Brett was in the bathroom, Jason brought him up.

I sighed as I grabbed a cupcake out of the container and started tearing off the top. "Oh well."

"Has he said anything to you, babe?" Kristen asked.

Jason shrugged. "He's been quiet. Not talking to anyone really. His door is usually shut, but he didn't show up again yesterday. I tried calling him early this morning about your party—it went straight to voice mail."

An uneasy feeling unfurled in my stomach, and apparently Kristen's too. "Should we be worried about him?" she asked as she tried to conceal her fear.

"I don't think so, he's just trying to figure some things

out, and doesn't know exactly how to react to all this yet. Like I said last weekend, he just needs time."

I frowned at Jason's words, how much time did he need? I understood things changing, but not calling me for my birthday? Not showing up? It was so unlike Eli.

"What are you doing?" Brett asked on a laugh.

I jumped at the sound of his voice suddenly behind me, and quickly forced my body to relax. "What do you mean?"

He pointed at the cupcake bottom sitting, forgotten about, on the island countertop, so I showed him the frosted part.

"I only eat the tops of cupcakes."

"Really? So the rest of the cake just gets left behind?"

My eyes widened and my breathing hitched. "Uh . . ."

He grabbed the cake sitting on the counter and popped a piece in his mouth. "I feel bad for the poor cake."

I slowly looked up to Kristen and Jason; both were staring at the rest of the cupcake like they didn't know what to say. And when Kristen looked up at me, that same look of pity she'd had for the last week was there.

It was ridiculous that I wanted to say that was Eli's part, that Brett couldn't eat it. Because Eli wasn't here, he'd made the decision not to be. I needed to accept that and move on.

Chapter Six

September 14, 2013

Paisley

JOGGING QUICKLY TO my front door a week later, I looked through the peephole, and a smile crossed my face as I opened the door.

"Good morning!"

Brett leaned forward to kiss my cheek as he stepped around me. "Hello, beautiful."

"Ha . . . I'm not so sure about that. I just woke up and I'm all gross."

Setting the two cups of coffee on the kitchen bar, he turned and pulled me close for a slower kiss. His tongue slid over mine in the most perfect, teasing way. "I'm not sure I agree with that," he countered.

"What's this?"

"That." He pulled back and made a face, like he wasn't sure how I'd respond. "You told me yesterday that you'd run of out coffee, and I figured you didn't go to the store after work . . . so I decided to bring you some. It was my excuse to come see you."

My smile widened, and I grabbed the cups before walking over to the couch, leaving the cups on the coffee table. "So you need an excuse to come see me now?"

"At eight A.M. on a Saturday? I figured I might." He grinned wryly and captured my lips again.

"Definitely don't need one," I assured him, and he laughed huskily.

He moved to kiss a slow line up my throat toward my mouth, and though I knew I should be embarrassed about the way my chest was moving roughly up and down, I couldn't think past the way his lips were making me feel to begin to. I moaned when he nipped on my bottom lip, and turned to bring one of my knees over his legs so I was sitting on his lap. His hands gripped at my back under my shirt as he claimed my mouth, and I rocked my hips against his hardening length, whimpering from the friction of his jeans against my sleep shorts.

"Paisley," he growled when I rocked against him again, but I didn't know if it was in warning, or begging me to continue.

I didn't stop.

We hadn't even gone this far yet, and something was

telling me I wasn't ready to sleep with him—but his lips drifting over and down my neck so he could kiss and bite on my collarbone, his large hands warming my skin wherever they touched, and his soft noises deep in his chest whenever I would move against him had me sitting up on my knees when his hands moved to the hem of my shorts.

There was a knock on my door that neither of us seemed to fully be aware of as my head tilted back and Brett's lips moved down my chest and fingers trailed the outside of my underwear.

The knocking got louder and my body jerked when the bell rang too.

Brett was breathing roughly and his dark green eyes were focused on my door before he looked up at me. "You expecting more company at eight on a Saturday morning?"

I shook my head and glanced behind me at the door where the hard knocking was still happening. "No."

"Do you want me to get it?" He no longer sounded curious; his voice was laced with alarm.

"No, it's fine." Scrambling off his lap, I worked at calming my racing heart as I walked quietly over to the door.

"Paisley," Brett warned, and suddenly he was off the couch and behind me.

When I looked through the peephole, my breath caught and I stumbled back a step into his arms.

"Christ, who is it?" He kept one arm around me, pulling me back as he stepped forward to look through the hole. His head jerked back when the knocking got louder, and I didn't blame him. If you didn't know Eli, he was terrifying to look at, and it sounded like he was a few knocks away from breaking down my door. "Do we need to call the cops or something?"

"No. He's my—well, he's my best friend."

Brett's eyebrows drew together, and he pointed at the door. "Is this Eli?"

I nodded at the same time Eli's rough voice came from the other side. "Paisley, please. I know you're here, I need to talk to you."

Brett looked confused, but didn't say anything else. He knew about my best friend, but he had no idea about the conversation I'd had with him two weeks ago. He had no idea I'd been in love with him for a dozen years.

He also had no idea we'd had a falling out. Because if Eli were still my best friend, he wouldn't be sitting there pounding on my door. He would've used his key and walked right in.

"I'll, uh, give you a moment?"

I nodded and watched Brett walk over to the coffee table to grab his cup before moving toward the kitchen. With a deep breath in, I unlocked and opened the door.

"Paisley," Eli breathed, and everything in me ached. I instantly wanted to cry all over again just looking at him. "God, Pay, I'm so sorry."

"It has been two weeks," I gritted out.

Eli seemed to hunch in on himself, and his face showed an exhaustion I couldn't begin to imagine. "I know, and I'm sorry. I just got back from Texas last night after being there for a week, and I couldn't let myself call you once I realized everything. Because I knew the second I heard your voice I would say it all, and you need to hear this in person."

He started to walk inside, so I moved around the door and mostly shut it behind me so I was blocking his way. Eli's brows drew together, and I just shook my head. "It's really not a good time right now."

It took a few seconds before understanding crossed his features. "He's here? Did he stay the night?" His chest's movements got more exaggerated, and his blue eyes narrowed.

Eli was about to explode.

"I think you should go."

"Did. He. Stay."

"You don't have the right to know that anymore, Eli. You made this decision. You decided there wouldn't be anything between us, and then you threw our friendship away."

His face softened and he stepped closer. "I never wanted to throw our friendship away, Pay. You're my best friend; you always will be. The thought of losing you kills me. I haven't talked to you because I thought you wouldn't want to hear from me after that, and I didn't even know what to say to you. I felt like the biggest kind of asshole and I didn't know how to face you after what I'd put you through for years. But, Paisley, I don't regret any of that nearly as much as I regret not realizing I was in love with you long before now."

My lips parted on a nearly inaudible gasp, and the ache inside me grew at hearing Eli say those words. Words I had been craving from him for twelve years.

His large hands cupped my cheeks and tilted my head back to look at him. "I love you, Paisley Morro. I'm *in* love with you. I can't lose you."

I'd wanted this, waited for this, and dreamt about this day for years. But after talking with Jason and Kristen . . . after two weeks of nothing from him . . . I couldn't tell if the passion and honesty in his voice was sincere, or something my mind was making up. As much as it killed me, I shook my head and stepped away from his grasp.

"You're just saying that because you want your wing-man back, Eli. I can't be her anymore. I'm sorry."

"Paisley—"

"Please, go home." Stepping into my apartment, I shut and locked the door, and stood there for long seconds as I tried to compose myself. When I turned around, Brett was standing a few feet away watching me, and I knew from his expression that he'd heard every word. "I guess I should explain that," I whispered.

With a sad smile, he nodded and turned to follow me to the couch, then sat stiffly as he waited for the story.

September 20, 2013

Eli

I LOOKED UP when a sandwich was dropped on my desk, and shot Jason a glare before I went back to working.

"You're welcome for feeding you."

"Thanks," I mumbled.

"You look like shit."

"Appreciate it."

"I knew this was going to happen," he continued, and I sat back in my desk chair and sighed.

"So you're coming in here to throw it in my face now? That's what this is?" I held my hands out and shrugged. "Go for it. Say, 'I told you so.' Tell me how you tried to warn me that I was going to lose my best friend."

He raised an eyebrow at me and unwrapped his sandwich. "Looks like you're telling yourself that enough for me. So I'll just sit here and eat."

"Nice," I sneered.

"Everyone's going to O'Malley's tonight, are you going to show?"

I rubbed at my aching temples and closed my eyes. "Why wouldn't I?"

"Because you've been hiding ever since she told you how she felt. You've been gone from everything we normally do the last couple weeks—I don't know *why* I would *possibly* think you wouldn't show."

"I was gone for a week dealing with shit you wouldn't understand. And before that, my best friend had blown my world and I felt like shit for everything I'd ever done to her. I didn't know how to be around her then."

"And now?"

My eyes lifted to meet his and I swallowed roughly. "And now she's moving on with her life, and I'm too late."

Jason was quiet for a long time after that as he ate his sandwich. I still hadn't touched mine by the time he asked, "What made you finally realize you were in love with her?"

I didn't know if Paisley had told Kristen and Jason, or if he just guessed it by the way I'd been acting this whole week, but I wasn't surprised by his question. "Last week I almost lost one of my sisters and my dad, both within twenty-four hours. I hated that with all that bullshit going on I felt like I couldn't even call Paisley to tell her what was happening. I hated that I'd already lost her. And it hurt—it hurt so much more than I could've ever imagined it would. Then my sister said something in reference to her fiancé, and it all just clicked. You remember how you told me I would be losing my best friend, not just my wingman?"

Jason nodded as he stared at me intently.

"My sister Rachel said something about the other half of her soul. And I knew it right then. The pain, feeling like nothing would be right again, all of it. I just thought to myself that I'd lost the girl who could touch my soul. I knew I was in love with her, and couldn't think of a time when I wasn't in love with her."

"Then tell her!"

I eyed him uncertainly. "Has she not talked to Kristen this week? I went over there on Saturday. Told her how I felt . . . she thought I was just saying it to get my wingman back. That guy was there; she wouldn't even let me in. Talked to me outside and then ran back in without letting me defend what I'd told her."

Jason nodded like he wasn't even realizing he was doing the movement. "Brett was there?"

"Yeah. I tried to walk in and she closed the door a bit, but she was still standing in the doorway so I could see in. I don't know how long he was there, but when Pay told me to go and was shutting the door, I looked up and he was a few feet behind her glaring at me."

Jason was quiet for a minute, but it was obvious he was trying to figure out if he should say what he was thinking. "He seems like a great guy and he's nice, but not in a way that's so perfect that you can hate him either. He even has an accent that Kristen can't stop talking about. But he kept rubbing me the wrong way. Every time a guy hugged Paisley at her birthday party, swear to God I thought Brett was going to rip Paisley away from them."

My brow pinched together. "What do you mean?"

"I mean he looked fucking pissed that she was touching another guy, but as soon as the look was there, it was gone again."

"Did you tell Kristen or Pay?"

"Kristen. She thinks I'm seeing things because I'm trying to find something about Brett not to like. Which—I don't know—might be true. We all wanted you with her, and I still do even though I'm not sure if you deserve her after how you treated her for all those years; but right now it doesn't matter because the girls are acting like Brett walks on water. Which means you're screwed."

I groaned into my hands and leaned the chair back so I was looking up at the ceiling when I moved my hands away. "Did you know?"

"About Brett?"

"No. Did you know she was in love with me?"

He let out a long sigh. "To be honest, I think you're the only one who didn't know, Eli."

I sat down so I was facing him again and gave him a look. "Why didn't you say something?"

"Besides the fact that my wife is one of her best friends, and they both made me swear, and I don't feel like sleeping on the couch? *You* should have seen it. I wanted to tell you a thousand times because I hated watching the way you crushed her with every girl you picked up, or dodged by using Paisley. But I kept telling myself if everyone else could see it in her, then surely her best friend would be able to see how much he was killing her."

"Twist that knife a little more," I whispered, and rubbed at my chest.

"Happy to. You're fucking dumb. You should have noticed how much she meant to you a long time ago, and you deserve to go through this pain for a few weeks when she went through it for years."

I glared up at him. "Anything else?"

"Are you letting her go?"

"Fuck no. She's mine," I growled.

He stood with a smile on his face. "Then I guess I'm done here. See you tonight."

September 20, 2013

Paisley

I ROLLED MY head to the side as Brett kissed my neck, and bit my lip when he nipped at the sensitive spot behind my ear.

"Are you hearing anything I'm saying?"

I shook my head at Kristen and smiled lazily. "Nope, what were . . . you . . . Kristen?" I took in her wide eyes and stiff posture, and turned to see what she was looking at.

My entire body froze, and feeling the way I'd stiffened, Brett stopped whispering in my ear and turned to look as well.

Eli was standing there across the table from us, his eyes glued to Brett and me.

Jason broke the awkward tension as he clapped Eli's shoulder. "Sit down, glad you could make it."

Eli didn't sit, and Brett's body seemed to get tighter and tighter. "Shit," he whispered, and stood, extending his arm. "I'm Brett." When Eli didn't move or say anything, he continued, "You're Eli. I've heard a lot about you from Paisley."

Eli finally tore his eyes from me to look at him, but his expression was unreadable. Shaking Brett's hand firmly, he raised an eyebrow. "Sorry to say I haven't heard much about you."

Brett smirked and cocked his head as he sat down. "Can't imagine why," he said dryly.

This wasn't happening.

"This is awkward, we need pitchers!" Kristen called out, and looked around for a waitress.

When no one came to our table, and no one had said another word, Brett pressed his lips to my temple. "I'll go." I gripped his hand harder when he started to stand, and he bent close to my ear again. "Just try to talk. I'll be back, love."

Eli's eyes never left mine, something I know Brett didn't miss by the way his eyes lingered on the back of Eli's head as he walked past him toward the bar.

"Pay," Eli's deep voice rumbled a minute after Brett walked away.

My chest burned, and my body was so tense I was positive I'd shatter if anyone touched me right now. But I ached for that voice. My eyes wanted to shut as it washed over me, and I knew goose bumps were covering my arms as a thousand different memories with Eli flashed through my mind.

"We need to talk," he urged.

"Why didn't you show up for her birthday?" Kristen bit out. "Or call?"

"Kristen," Jason warned.

"I was in Texas. My sister was almost killed. Little bit of a family emergency." Every word was clipped and sounded like it was coming from a robot. But it still got through to me.

Remembering his voice mail, my eyes widened. "Oh my God. Rachel? Is she okay?"

"She's going to be fine." Finally moving his eyes away from me, he glanced at Kristen for a few seconds. "I called Paisley that day."

"He did?" she asked me.

I was back to trying to hold my rigid body together again now that Eli's dark eyes were piercing into mine, but I somehow managed to nod. "He left a message, I didn't know about it until after you were all gone . . . and it hadn't explained anything other than he was in Texas because of Rachel."

When Eli spoke again, his voice was devoid of emotion—but his eyes were telling me a hundred things. Things I couldn't handle right now. "But that's not why I want to talk to you," he insisted.

I shook my head and tried to steady my shaking jaw. "I can't talk to you about that," I managed to whisper just as Brett came back.

After setting a pitcher down on the table, he put a glass of Guinness in front of Eli, and my eyes widened. I'd mentioned that in passing.

Looking at Brett, I wasn't sure what I expected to find. Him smirking because he was trying to look better in front of me? Instead, his expression was solemn as he came to sit next to me.

His eyes darted to Eli once he was in his chair, and following his line of sight, my breath got caught in my throat to find him still intently watching me. Everything about Eli's exterior screamed that he was ready to fight somebody—anybody. But his eyes were pleading with me to listen to him.

I couldn't. I was sure if I did, I would want to believe him. I would forget about the years of heartache. I would do anything he asked me to.

Looking back over to Brett, I hated when I found him watching me too, his expression barely concealing his sadness.

I couldn't sit here anymore. Not with these two men here.

One who was taking my heart, the other who still owned my soul.

Standing quickly, I ignored everyone calling my name and escaped from the bar and into the parking lot. Once I was outside, my steps turned into sprints until I reached Brett's car. Bending over, I pressed my hands against my knees and took in staggering breaths.

It hadn't been a far run, but I felt like I couldn't breathe. It felt like I'd been holding my breath from the moment Eli had walked in. It felt like I was about to break.

"Come here," Brett commanded gently, and pulled me upright so he could wrap his arms around me.

A hard sob burst from my chest, and my body began trembling violently—and I hated that he was seeing this.

Because he knew what this was, he knew who these tears were for, and that they had absolutely nothing to do with us.

"It's okay, sweetheart. It's going to be okay," he crooned, and pressed his lips to the top of my head.

I gripped on to his shirt as I buried my head against his chest and cried. I didn't understand how he could say that. Not now, not when he was caught in the middle of this and knew exactly what was going on. I shook my head quickly as I tried to pull in air, and Brett stood there calmly running his hand over my back.

"Come on, Paisley, I'll take you home."

"But—"

"This is hard for you, and you're upset. Let me take you home so you have time to be alone to think about all this. And when you're ready, you can come over and we'll talk through whatever you've decided."

I swallowed roughly. "No. Brett, no! I want to be with you."

His full lips fell onto mine to quiet anything else I would say, and when he pulled back, his green eyes held mine. "You loved him first," he said simply.

"But I'm—" I cut off and briefly debated whether or not to say the words that were begging to get out. With a weighted sigh, I admitted, "I'm falling in love with you."

Brett exhaled in a rush, and offered me a sad smile "Christ, Paisley, I wish I could've told you how I'm falling madly in love with you under different circumstances, but it's because I am that I have to give you this chance. All right?"

I nodded as more tears fell down my cheeks, and whimpered from the force of his next kiss.

"It's going to be okay. *You're* going to be okay," he whispered, then released me, and opened the passenger seat of his car.

As I slid into the car, I didn't know how I was supposed to choose between the two. There was no obvious answer to me. I'd never met a man like Brett, and he'd been slowly putting together the shattered pieces of me from years with Eli as he'd quickly embedded himself in my heart and life. But there was no getting over someone like Eli, and I wondered how much it would hurt to live the rest of my life without him—because it was clear I couldn't have both of them in my life. I wondered if the soul-deep ache would eventually fade, and if Eli would just become a fond memory as my first love, or if Kristen had been right, and I would always wonder what if.

Chapter Seven

September 21, 2013

Eli

PULLING MY TRUCK to a stop in front of Paisley's building, I rubbed at my eyes and cracked my neck before stepping out. I hadn't slept last night—not that I'd slept much in the last few weeks, but there'd been nothing last night. I'd tried propping up the pillows the way Paisley always did, but it wasn't the same without her.

I shut and locked the door behind me, and took slow steps toward her apartment as I tried to prepare myself for Brett being here again.

I knew I'd been an ass the night before, but seeing him

kissing her had my blood boiling and me straining not to throw something. Because that would have helped so much. *I'm gonna throw this heavy table, and you're gonna like it.* Paisley didn't want someone turning into a caveman while he fought for her. She wanted someone to love her the way she loved them. She wanted someone not to hurt her like I'd been doing.

A sharp inhale had me freezing and my head snapping up to see my Paisley standing there in front of me. Brown eyes wide and unsure, dark hair falling softly around her face and past her shoulders, too-full lips barely opened, and looking as short and perfect as ever.

She was perfect. Why had that taken me so long to notice?

"Paisley," I breathed.

"Why are you here?" she asked through clenched teeth.

"Because I love you, and I need—"

"You can't just decide that now that I'm trying to be happy, Eli! You can't come in and try to ruin this now that you're missing me," she seethed, but underneath that anger was so much sadness she was working at concealing.

"I *do* miss you, Pay," I admitted as I closed the distance between us. She took a few steps back, and I took another forward—capturing her face in my hands so she wouldn't try to keep moving. "But I'm not trying to ruin your happiness. I know I've done that more times than I can imagine . . . I know, and I'm so goddamn sorry."

"Language," she chastised softly.

"But this isn't about missing my wingman. This isn't about being afraid to lose my best friend to a guy like Brett. This is about realizing something I should have years ago, and being fucking terrified that I'm about to lose the best thing to ever happen to me."

She swallowed hard and tried to turn her head, and when my hands wouldn't let her, she shut her eyes.

"You *can't* do this to me, Eli," Paisley murmured. "I told you everything—I laid a decade worth of secrets and feelings out on the table, and you did not reciprocate one of those. I *get* that I kind of just threw everything on you all at once. I *get* that I blindsided you with my confession. But even if I got past you avoiding me for the following two weeks, and even if I could forget what you told me outside of Grind, I will never be able to forget how horrified you looked when I told you that I loved you. And it's because of that image that is stuck in my mind that I can't believe what you're saying now—no matter how much I want to."

Paisley hadn't once opened her eyes throughout that, and somehow that fact made this harder. Because it just confirmed how badly I'd hurt her if she couldn't even look at me while she said those things.

My breaths came heavily as I tried to find the words to say for her to understand how serious I was about this—about us. I wished I'd thought of something before I came over here and started fumbling my words to the point where I was sure I was making it worse.

"I want *you*, Paisley. I want your propped-up pillows that I hate so damn much, but know you can't sleep without. I want to split milkshakes and cupcakes with you so I don't have to choose one flavor and don't have to eat the frosting. I want Sunday mornings with you *every* morning for the rest of our lives, because any day that starts with you is perfect. I want to always give you the first bite of my food, because I know the first bite of anything is your favorite. I want you to always get annoyed when I cuss because that face you make when I do is one of my favorites."

Tears slipped from her closed eyes. The sight made it feel like someone was gripping my heart and slowly squeezing.

"I never want to make you cry again unless they're happy tears. I want to know you so much better than I already do. I want to know where to kiss and touch you to make your eyes close. I want to know what to do to make you moan my name. I want to finally understand why you hate cussing so much. I want to know what you want for your future, and I want to be the one to give it to you. I love you, and I want to spend every day for the rest of my life loving you, Paisley. I'm sorry it took me so long, but please don't take you from me."

A few seconds passed without a response from her before she said, "I have to go."

"Paisley—"

"Please, let me go," she whimpered, and finally her eyes opened.

"I can't do that," I replied honestly.

A weighted breath left her, and she brought her small hands up to remove mine. "You need to learn how."

I knew we weren't talking about physically, and I wasn't ready for this. I couldn't let her go—I couldn't lose her. "Don't ask me to do that."

She couldn't have moved me no matter how hard she tried, but my hands still fell from her face when she shook her head and said, "I'm sorry."

My arms fell heavily to my sides, and I stared at the sidewalk as she moved around me to leave. I wanted to keep fighting for her, I wanted to keep showing her how much I wanted this, but I was afraid that all I was doing was hurting her. And after finding out that I'd been doing exactly that for years—I wasn't sure I could force myself to hurt her any more.

September 21, 2013

Paisley

I STARED AT the ocean; my entire body felt numb as I tried to think through what I wanted. I'd been on my way to Brett's to talk to him when I ran into Eli, sure that I would tell Brett I wanted to continue a relationship with him. But now I was back to not being sure of anything. Neither seemed like the better choice, and, still, neither seemed like the obvious choice. There was nothing wrong with Brett other than he wasn't Eli, and while I couldn't use the years of Eli breaking my heart against him, I *could* use the past few weeks.

Like I'd told him, no matter how much I wanted to believe his words now, I couldn't. While they were more than I'd ever wanted from him, there was still that fear that he was saying everything because he didn't want to lose his best friend.

I sat there for hours with my arms wrapped tightly around my waist as I tried to hold myself together, and fought with myself over who I couldn't live without.

In a daze, I stood from my spot and walked back to my car before driving to Brett's. I still didn't know who I would choose. All I knew was the way I'd felt when I'd seen Eli walking toward me this morning, and how much it had hurt to walk away from him. As I walked to Brett's door, I told myself that I'd know who I couldn't live without the moment I saw him, and then I would make my choice.

Knocking on his door, I took calming breaths as I waited for him to answer. Part of me was afraid to find out who I wanted to spend the rest of my life with—but I knew I couldn't continue to do this to them or myself.

"Hey," Brett said as he opened the door.

Looking into his worried green eyes, the pressure was already lessening on my chest—making it easier to breathe. Like it always did, the pain from being near Eli was slowly fading as I stood in front of Brett. And I knew that I'd somehow fallen in love with this man in a matter of weeks, no matter how insane that seemed.

And I also knew I had my answer.

A sharp cry burst from my chest and I slapped my

hand over my mouth to quiet it, and understanding covered his face.

"Oh, Paisley," he whispered. Wrapping his arms around my shoulders, he pulled me into his chest as he shut the door behind us.

September 21, 2013

Eli

I GOT UP from where I'd spent the last five hours lying on the couch and walked slowly into the kitchen. I knew I should probably eat, but nothing sounded good. I'd talked to Jason a couple hours ago, and since I knew Paisley wasn't with Kristen, that only left one other person I could think she'd spend a Saturday with.

And it was killing me.

I wanted to go wait at her apartment so I could try to talk to her again, but even Kristen and Jason thought it was a bad idea. They thought it was time I started backing off. I knew they were right; I just wasn't ready to admit it.

Opening the fridge, I grabbed a beer and turned to walk back to the couch, but stopped when a knock sounded on my door. I stood there staring at it for a few moments while I tried to figure out if I should answer or act like I wasn't here.

I didn't need Jason telling me how much I'd fucked up again. I already knew.

When the knock came again, I set the beer down on the table and walked over to the door. Unlocking and opening it without bothering to see who it was, I froze when I saw Paisley standing there, tears streaming down her face.

"Pay—"

"Please tell me I made the right decision in choosing you."

"What?" I asked on a breath, and curled my arms around her when she crushed her body to mine.

She swallowed roughly and looked up at me. "I can live without him—I can't live without you."

A smile pulled at my lips for the first time in weeks, and then I did something I should have done long ago. Bending low, I brought my face within a breath of hers to whisper, "I love you, Paisley Morro." before pressing my lips to hers.

Her arms slowly moved around my neck, holding me closer as I prompted her lips open with mine. Wrapping my arms tightly against her waist, I straightened and pressed her back against the wall, loving the throaty sound she made as I did. Her hands moved through my hair as her legs tightened around my hips, and her chest heaved when I pulled back from the kiss.

Using the wall and one arm to hold her up, I kept my eyes on hers, watching as they widened when I made a slow line down her throat with the tips of my fingers. My lips tilted up on one side when a shiver moved through her body, and I leaned forward to make the same line with my lips and teeth. Her head dropped back against the wall, and a soft, breathy whimper sounded from her chest. I decided right then that was my favorite sound in the world.

"I want to hear you say it again."

"I chose you," she breathed, her declaration sounding almost like a question.

Moving away from her neck, I waited until she lowered her head to look at me again. "Not that, Pay."

"I love you?" she asked softly.

"Yeah."

Her lips curved up into a bright smile and her brown eyes searched my face for a few silent seconds. "I love you, Eli."

I took a deep breath in as her words washed over me, and thanked God for giving me this second chance with her.

"And I want propped-up pillows with you."

A hard laugh left me and I pressed my mouth firmly to hers. "And?"

"And Sunday mornings every morning."

"And?" I prompted, eager to hear everything else I'd wanted from her this morning.

"I want to watch you roll your eyes every time I get on you for cussing, even though you know it's coming."

"And?"

"And I want to take the first bite of all your food," she said against my lips then bit down on the bottom one.

"And?" I growled.

"And I want the frosted half of your cupcakes. And to share milkshakes with you. And for you to force me to change when you hate what I'm wearing." Pulling back a fraction of an inch from my face, she pressed her palms to my cheeks and spoke softly. "And I want to love you, and be loved by you, every day for the rest of our lives."

Resting my forehead against hers, I closed my eyes and let out a relieved breath. "All of that, Pay. Forever."

September 21, 2013

Paisley

MY EYES STAYED locked on Eli's as he walked us to his bedroom, and my heart began hammering as the possibilities of what we were about to do flooded my mind. Things I'd dreamt of for years were now finally about to become a reality.

Placing one knee on the bed, he lowered our bodies onto the comforter—keeping his body a few inches above mine once I had unwrapped myself from him. My pulse thrummed violently when he smiled before dipping his head to kiss his way down my throat the same way he'd done in the entryway. I brought my knees up to curl around his hips, and had to bite down on my lip to keep from making any noises when he rested himself between my legs. Using his teeth to gently pull my lip free, he kissed the spot I'd been biting down on before sliding his tongue into my mouth to torture me with unhurried strokes.

Moving my hands up his muscled forearms, my fingers curled around his straining upper arms before sliding over his chest and down his stomach. Even through the material of his shirt I could feel the muscles in his stomach twitch from my touch, and with shaky hands, I pressed my fingers to the skin just above his shorts.

A growl rumbled in his chest, and his body moved a fraction closer. I curled my fingers against his skin, and suddenly his body was off mine and he was sitting next to me. Blue eyes dark with want, chest rising and falling quickly.

"I'm sorry," I said automatically. I didn't know what I'd done, but I knew whatever had just happened had to have been because of me.

"Don't apologize," he begged. "I can't do this with you yet. Not when you just showed up here after there's been so much between us that was unknown. Not when I've hurt you for twelve years, and still have so much to apologize for. Not when I don't know what's going on with Brett or when you were last with him."

My forehead creased in confusion. "I just came from— Wait, like *with* him with him?" When Eli didn't respond, I sat up and turned to face him. "I never did anything with Brett."

"But he was at your apartment last week when I showed up . . ."

Was it ridiculous that I was fighting back a smile? It was so weird to have Eli look like *I'd* crushed *him*. "And he hadn't even gotten there five minutes before. He brought me coffee. We kissed, and that's it—your visit last week made things kind of awkward between us."

"That's not one of the things I'm going to apologize for."

I made a face and sighed. "Last night when I left O'Malley's, he came out there to take me home. He told me to think about everything over the weekend, and when I was ready, to go talk to him. He looked crushed because he'd already seen me cry over you too many times, and I think he knew that I wouldn't choose him." Looking into Eli's eyes, I moved closer and he pulled me onto his lap, but his expression was subdued as he waited for me to continue. "I wanted to choose him, Eli. I wanted to, and I told him that . . . I freaked when he told me to think about things, because I knew what that implied. And you know what he said?"

Eli raised one eyebrow, but didn't speak. I think he was forcing himself not to, judging by the way his fingers were curling around me like he wasn't about to let me go for anything.

"He said, 'You loved him first,' like that should have answered everything. He didn't want to compete with you even though I was with him. He didn't want to compete with a guy who knew me better than I knew myself." Swallowing past the tightness in my throat, I tried to stop the way my body wanted to curl in on itself. "I was on my way to tell him I'd chosen him this afternoon when you stopped me, but after I left you, I went to the beach instead and sat there for hours. When I finally got up to drive to his place, I still didn't know who I would choose, and I didn't know until he opened his door."

Eli's eyes hardened. "What did he do?"

I ran my fingers through his hair to calm him and shook my head subtly. "Nothing. And everything. He made it easier to breathe. He made the ache of talking to you go away. I knew when I looked at him that I'd somehow fallen in love with him, and I knew loving him could be easy. But the way he made me feel didn't compare to the way I'd instantly felt whole as soon as you were near me. Or how I'd felt like I was dying while I walked away from you because I'd known you wouldn't be a part of my life. He knew the second I realized who my choice was, and I know I broke his heart. He held me for a long time, and he asked what made me decide."

"Did you tell him?"

I nodded and placed a hand over his chest. "I said, 'I can see a future with you . . . but I can't see one without him.' And he and I both knew that if he was in my future, you wouldn't be."

"I'm sorry you're hurting, and I'm sorry I put you in this position, Paisley."

I cracked a tiny smile and forced a laugh. "It would've been a lot easier if you'd figured out you loved me a long time ago."

Eli didn't find that amusing.

"I told you before, you own my soul. No one can touch a love like that."

He brushed back hair that had fallen in my face,

and his blue eyes followed the movement before meeting mine again. "I don't know what I did to deserve your love, Paisley, but I'm thankful for it." Pressing his lips to mine gently, he only pulled back enough to say, "I'm sorry for not knowing. I'm sorry for using you as a shield from exes, and using you to get other girls when I should have known that you were the only girl who mattered."

"Eli—"

"I'm sorry for making you watch me with anyone else when it always should have been you. I'm sorry for hurting you over and over again."

"Stop!" I pled. "Stop, Eli, I know you are. But we need to move past that or you're going to keep tearing yourself up over what's in the past. And I want to start a future with you."

"You don't understand how much I hate—"

"Then let me apologize for taking so long to tell you," I begged, cutting him off.

His head jerked back. "What? No."

"Yes," I argued. "None of this would've happened if I'd just told you a long time ago."

"But you don't know if that would have changed things then. You don't know if our friendship would've been different. We might not have ended up like we are now."

I hadn't thought of it that way, and based on the look Eli was giving me, my expression was saying just that.

"So as long as you don't try to take blame, I'll . . . *try* to stop apologizing," he promised, and I narrowed my eyes at him. He shook his head slowly when he knew I was getting ready to argue that too. "That's the best you're getting, Paisley. I've had to watch you cry numerous times because of me. I've beat guys up over you for a lot less than that."

"*Guys* as in plural?"

"Yeah." He breathed the word like that shouldn't be news. It was.

"Do I want to—"

"No."

I bit back a smile and rolled my eyes. "Got it."

Pushing me off his lap, he kissed me forcefully as he climbed off the bed. "I'm gonna lock up, and I'm not letting you leave. So change, because I'm exhausted and I want you in my arms."

My heart took off and his face lit up in reaction to the cheesiest smile that was covering my own. I'd slept in a bed with him hundreds of times, but everything was different now, and he'd just told me he wanted me in his arms. And he'd been kissing me. Not fake brushes of his lips against the side of my neck for girls to see, but actual kisses that I'd only dreamt of. That's it. I had to be dreaming.

I'm going to wake up and all of this will be some sick joke.

"It's real, Pay."

I looked up to where he was standing in the doorway, and my eyebrows drew together.

"You look like you're starting to freak out, and I'm thinking the same thing. That's why I'm falling asleep with you in my arms tonight. Because I need to feel you and be able to touch you to know that this isn't all going to be gone in the morning."

My lips parted and I blinked slowly at him. "I don't know if I should be in awe, or kinda creeped out that you can read my mind now."

He shrugged and turned to walk down the hall, his voice trailing behind him. "Or you just said it out loud."

My expression fell even though he couldn't see me anymore. Jerk.

Scrambling quickly off the bed, I pulled my pants and shirt off, and folded them in a pile next to Eli's dresser. Grabbing one of his shirts out of the drawers, I started to put it on, and at the last second, took my bra off. It's not like I needed the bra that much, but I still usually wore one if I knew I'd be sleeping with him.

Slipping the shirt over my head, I let it fall over my body and pulled my hair out of the collar.

You always look like such a lost little girl when you're in my clothes.

I froze on my way back to his bed when I remembered the words he'd told me a few months ago, and looked down at where his shirt hung almost to my knees. I didn't want to look like a little girl, and I wanted to wear his shirt. I always wore them when we slept together . . . never mind the fact that I didn't have anything else to wear.

Grabbing the bottom of his shirt, I pulled together the loose material and tied it all in a knot against the side of my thigh. By the time I straightened, his shirt looked a lot more like the shirt-dress Kristen had made me wear than one of Eli's baggy shirts I always drowned in. It sat just under my butt and tight against my thighs, and from the way Eli stopped walking and his eyes widened as they took me in, I knew that "lost little girl" wasn't anywhere in his vocabulary right now.

Keeping his eyes on me, he pulled his shirt over his head and let it fall to the floor as his hands went to the button on his dark tan cargo shorts. My mind knew I should have turned away, that I wasn't supposed to watch Eli when he changed—but that'd been before.

My lips felt dry when he stood from taking off his shorts, and I couldn't stop myself from finally looking at his wide, muscular build in nothing but a tight pair of dark boxer briefs as he walked toward me. A smirk played on his lips as he moved past me, and I turned to watch the muscles in his back move as he bent to prop up all the pillows.

"Are you—" I cleared my throat. "Are you not putting on shorts?"

He looked over his shoulder, that same smirk still taunting me. "Are you going to fix my shirt?"

"No."

"If I'm going to be tortured by the sight of you like that, Paisley, I'm not helping you by putting anything else on."

"But I'm covered! Well, half of me is."

"No one ever said you had to be." He pulled back the comforter and slid into the bed, messing with the pillows as he tried to get comfortable sitting up against them.

I just stood there staring at him with my jaw dropped.

"Bed, Paisley."

His words moved straight to my stomach and curled in the most amazing way. It didn't matter that I'd seen him in a bed hundreds of times like he was then; looking at him like this with those words was something right from one of my fantasies. And while I wanted to live out those fantasies so bad, I also kind of wanted to draw out this whole torturing him. He'd tortured me for years; it was an exhilarating feeling knowing I was finally getting my chance.

I walked over to the bed and crawled on, but instead of getting on my side and curling up against him, I climbed onto his lap. Trying to ignore the way his eyes heated so I wouldn't go right into fantasy mode, I reached back for the comforter and pulled it over my shoulders as I rested myself against his chest with my cheek pressed to his shoulder.

Eli's hands went to my hips and began moving back, but paused. "Paisley," he growled in warning.

"You should've put your shorts on."

He leaned his head back against the pillows and laughed in frustration. "You're making it a lot harder than it needs to be."

"Pun intended?" With how short I'd made the shirt, all that was between us was two thin pieces of cotton, and I involuntarily rocked my hips against his growing erection.

"Fuck," he groaned, and tried to still my hips.

"Language."

Gripping my chin between his fingers, he moved my head so he could look in my eyes. "Who was the last?" he demanded.

My breathing deepened as I pressed myself more firmly against him. "Johnny Gallo," I responded automatically.

"That first time?"

I nodded and moved against him again, a whimper on the tip of my tongue, but Eli's hand flexed against my hip to the point where it got my attention.

"Who was the last guy to touch you?"

Heat flooded my cheeks, and I sat there staring at him for long seconds. I only responded when his fingers left my chin and brushed against my cheek.

"Paisley," he crooned. "Tell me."

"No one."

His eyebrows slammed down. "Not even Johnny?" When I shook my head, he muttered something too low for me to hear. "Tomorrow's Sunday. Starting tomorrow, everything is going to be about you."

"What?"

Bringing his mouth to mine, he spoke against it. "For one week, I'm going to show you what it feels like to be touched . . . *everywhere*. The week after I am going to explore every inch of you with my tongue," he vowed, and a bone-deep shiver moved through my body. "And when that week is up, I'm going to spend an entire day buried deep inside you."

And I'd thought it was my turn to be the torturer. My breaths were so ragged my voice was nearly inaudible. "That's not necessary."

"I disagree." Capturing my mouth with his, he stopped any other protests I may have had as he kissed me thoroughly. "Now go to sleep before I try to think of reasons why right now isn't a bad idea."

I sagged against his chest, and a deep laugh filled the room. All he'd done was told me everything, and I was already aching for him and exhausted from what he'd promised. I was sure I wouldn't sleep after that with how wild my mind was running, but his deep, rhythmic breaths soon had my eyes shutting and I slowly fell asleep on his lap.

Chapter Eight

September 22, 2013

Paisley

"PAISLEY."

My eyes cracked open to Eli's dark room hours later, and I rolled my head back to see him looking down at me. "Hi," I said hoarsely.

"Hey." He smiled. "Guess what."

"Hmm?"

"It's Sunday."

I was still asleep enough that I had no idea what he was talking about until his lips were pressed against mine and his hands were moving down my back.

It was Sunday. Holy crap, it was Sunday.

Running his hands down the curve of my back and over my butt, he curled his fingers around the hem of his shirt on my body to pull it higher. There was no time for worry about where this was going—there was no reason to think of anything other than the way his hands felt on my bare skin . . . I'd wanted this for as long as I could remember.

Sitting up straighter, I threaded my fingers in his hair as I deepened the kiss, muting my moan when his long fingers pulled aside my underwear and trailed over me. A shiver coursed through my body when his thumb circled against my clit, and I had to break away from our kiss when it became too difficult to remember how to breathe.

I pressed my forehead against his and kept my fingers locked in his hair as I moved my hips against his hand, my movements stopping when he slowly slid one finger inside me.

"You okay?"

I lowered myself slightly, and bit my lip against the feel of him. "More," I whimpered, and before I could be embarrassed about my plea, he was adding a second finger and I was trying to stifle a gasp.

I hadn't meant *that* by more. I'd meant I wanted more of his teasing, more of his fingers and palm moving against me . . . but, oh God, when he began moving them in and out of me, I thought I'd died and gone to heaven.

My stomach tightened and my body warmed as I rocked against his hand, and soon the tightening got to be too much, but even as I stopped moving and my body became as tight as a bow, Eli's hand continued the sweetest agony I'd ever endured. I tried to say his name, but my breath was caught in my throat and my blood felt like it was on fire.

Pressing the heel of his palm against my clit, he tightened his grip on my hip at the same time, and it felt like everything in me shattered. No sound left me as my body shook against the rush of adrenaline, but my mouth remained open as I desperately tried to pull in air.

Eli's movements slowed, and my body jerked when he ran his fingers over my clit as he removed his hand. "Happy Sunday," he murmured against my neck, then placed a kiss there.

His hands wrapped around my thighs to pull me closer onto his lap, and I whimpered when his thick erection pressed against me. Releasing the lock I had on his hair, I sat back and began trailing my fingers down his chest. And even though everything was too sensitive, I couldn't stop myself from rocking against him, and wishing there wasn't any material between us.

"No, Pay." He stopped my hands when they reached his stomach, and pulled them to our sides.

"What? Why?"

His eyes—darkened from the room—held mine, and the heat was clear there. I didn't have to be sitting on his lap to know what he wanted. "I told you these next two weeks were about you."

"But, Eli—"

"Don't fight me on this, Pay. I will get my way," he

assured me, the husky tone of his voice caused another shiver to move up my spine. "Go back to sleep."

I'd just had my first orgasm caused by someone other than myself, my body was still shaking from the aftereffects, and I was sitting on his lap and knew this had to be killing him. I so did not want to go to sleep.

Gripping his hands tightly, I pressed down on his lap harder and ground my hips against him.

His eyes flew open. "Paisley," he said in warning, but I didn't stop.

Releasing my hands, he pushed up the shirt I was wearing even higher and gripped the top of my underwear. With one hard tug, and a shocked cry from me, he tore the material off my body and threw it off the side of the bed.

I couldn't even be mad. I was incredibly turned on by it and high off the fact that I was about to get what I wanted.

I inhaled sharply when he pressed his fingers inside me, and trembled when he whispered darkly, "I warned you."

Removing his hand, he gripped my bottom and pressed me onto his lap again, this time helping in my movements. He groaned and buried his head against my neck, and when my hands reached for his boxer briefs again, his fingers gripping my butt spread my cheeks, and one of his fingers pushed against a place no person should ever touch.

"Eli!" I screeched, and sat up, trying to get away from the invasion.

A soft laugh rumbled in his chest, and one of his hands moved back to my clit. "I told you to go to sleep, Pay."

I arched my back, trying to find more pressure while simultaneously shaking my head. "That's—no. Just . . . no."

"Are you sure?" he asked as his other hand gently touched my bottom.

"Y-yes."

"Lean against my chest again, Paisley." When I didn't move from my straightened position, his hand moved from my bottom to press two fingers deep inside me. "Trust me."

I slowly lowered myself; my eyes were already fluttering shut with how different everything felt in this position. I bit down on my bottom lip and curled my arms around his shoulders as I tried to hold on. It felt like at any second I would be lost—but being lost in Eli didn't sound like a bad thing.

My breathing turned ragged when I got closer to another orgasm; my mind was so consumed in the feel I didn't notice Eli switching which fingers were inside me until one was pushing against no-man's-land again.

I stiffened and wanted to get away from it again, but I was so close, and Eli's calming voice had me staying where I was.

"Trust me, Pay."

His finger pushed in slowly as I kept moving against him, and my face tightened against the foreign pressure. "Please," I whimpered.

But I didn't know what I was begging for. Please stop. Please *don't* stop. Because the pressure was still building—faster now, and I found myself pressing back against him instead of trying to get away from him.

"God, Eli, please."

Too much. Too much. He was everywhere, and I knew if I let go, it was all going to be too much.

When it felt like I couldn't take any more of him, the pressure on my clit increased and I came with a sharp cry. It wasn't like before. It didn't feel like I was shattering. It felt like I was weightless, floating, nothing until everything came crashing down in a heavy rush that began in my stomach and spread all the way to my fingers and toes.

"Pay?" Eli asked softly a few moments later.

"Hmm?" I managed to force from my chest. My forehead was pressed to his neck, my cheek was against his collarbone, and my body was slumped against his as I waited to come back to earth.

"You okay?"

"That was . . . that . . ." I trailed off, and gave up on trying to explain the experience as well as my discomfort and pleasure with it.

"I need to know if you're okay," he prompted. When I just nodded, he chuckled and wrapped his arms tight around me. "Thank you for trusting me."

"Always," I muttered.

He held me until my eyes started drifting shut, and when I felt myself being moved, I blinked slowly up at him.

"Where are you going?"

Eli laughed huskily. "I'm gonna take a shower."

My eyes slid down to his erection, and I sat up on the bed. "Please, let me."

With a searing kiss, he laid me back down on the bed. "These weeks are about you, I can take care of me."

"Eli—"

"Sleep, Pay. I love you."

I watched him walk into the bathroom, and tried to tell myself to get up and go to him, but my eyes were already shutting again by the time I heard the water turn on.

September 22, 2013

Eli

SHUTTING THE FRONT door softly behind me, I took a few steps in the direction of my bedroom and listened for any movement. When there wasn't any, I turned and walked through my apartment and into my kitchen. Setting down the coffees and breakfast on the island, I sorted everything out before heading back toward my bedroom.

As I cracked open the door, my heart pounded against my chest when I saw Paisley lying on her stomach on my bed, right knee pulled up to the side.

Years of not seeing what was right in front of me . . . and somehow it still felt like I couldn't believe she was finally mine. Somehow I'd known what she meant to me. I'd known and had just been too stupid.

Crawling onto the bed, I knelt down above her and placed light kisses on the back of her neck, moving around to her cheek.

"Wake up, beautiful girl."

She squinted up at me for a second before closing her eyes again and trying to burrow under the comforter.

Brushing back her dark hair, wild from sleep, I let my lips trail across her exposed cheekbone and up over her eyebrow. "It's Sunday morning, I have coffee and breakfast."

"Sounding better," she mumbled.

"I'll give you the first bite?" I offered.

"Gettin' there."

"I need you to wake up so I can kiss you. It's been hours."

Her lips curved up in a smile. "Poor you."

Nibbling on her ear, I whispered, "And I have a lot of touching to do."

Red stained her porcelain cheeks when I leaned back, and her eyes were wide when she turned her head to look up at me. "Do you now?"

Keeping my weight on one arm, I pulled the comforter down enough so I could trail my free hand along her side until I got to where the shirt she was wearing had ridden up to her hips. Paisley pushed her ass up when I moved my hand between her and the bed, and as soon as I had my hands between her legs, she quickly wiggled away from the comforter and me, and jumped off the bed.

"What—"

She darted out of the room and down the hall, and I scrambled off the bed and took off after her. I found her standing in the kitchen taking a long drink from one of the coffee cups, and raised an eyebrow at her as I walked to stand behind her.

"So you run from me now?"

Tilting her head back so it was resting against my chest, she gave me a doe-eyed look. "You promised coffee and breakfast."

"I did."

"And then there were some things you wanted to do . . . so coffee and breakfast first."

I planted my chin on her head when she looked down to unwrap one of the sandwiches. "I didn't mean for those to be in order," I grumbled.

She handed me the sandwich after checking it. "Well, you got your way last night, so I'm getting my way this morning."

A slow grin crossed my face. "You enjoyed it."

Paisley stilled against my body. "That's embarrassing."

Tossing the sandwich back on the island, I turned her around and bent down to look directly in her eyes. "Did you enjoy it, yes or no? Because if you didn't, tell me now, Paisley, and I'll never do that to you again."

Her cheeks flushed again and she looked away for a second. "I did, I just—I don't know how to feel about the fact that I did. Like I said, it's embarrassing."

"Don't be embarrassed," I begged her. "It felt good for you, and I loved watching you come undone in my arms—that's all that matters."

"Still embarrassing," she muttered as she turned back around and grabbed for her own sandwich.

"You'll beg for it one day," I assured her.

"Eli!"

"What?"

"I would really like to eat, and I'm not going to be able to if you keep talking about that."

I was glad she couldn't see me smiling. Picking up my food, I unwrapped it and held it in front of her for her to take the first bite before taking my own.

"Pay, can I ask you something?" I asked when I'd finished my food.

She turned around and leaned against the island, and just raised an eyebrow as she chewed.

"Why do you get on me for cussing?"

Her expression fell and she worked at swallowing as she turned and grabbed for her coffee.

"When we were younger I thought you were a prude, but then as we got older I thought it was just more of a running joke for us. It wasn't until you cussed at me at the bar, and then everything went to shit, that I thought it might be something else. And I was just wondering if there *was* a reason."

She laughed hesitantly. "It is more of a joke now, but I still don't like it." I stood there waiting for her to continue, and after a couple minutes, she took a deep breath in and shrugged. "My dad was an alcoholic. It wasn't like he'd drink every night, thank God. But twice a week maybe? And when he drank, he drank enough to put ten men out for the night. Whatever he'd gone out to buy, he'd finish all of it every time. Mom hated that he drank, said he was blowing our money and trying to kill himself. She'd always start cussing at him. He hated cussing, and she knew it . . . but she'd keep throwing out words like she was goading him or something. Because he'd just yell louder and louder, telling her to stop cussing until he started throwing things at her or hitting her. And he'd hit her until one of them was unconscious."

"Paisley," I whispered, horrified. "How did I not know about this?"

Her brown eyes darted up to mine. "The funny thing about all this? He's a pastor, or was; I don't know what he's doing anymore. I haven't seen him since I was eleven. At church on Sunday we were the picture-perfect family for the congregation, but when he'd get the itch to drink . . . he'd go a few towns over to a liquor store and it would start all over again. I think that's why my mom provoked him with the cussing, because she felt like she couldn't just leave a man who would drink himself to sleep a couple nights a week and leave us without any money . . . she wanted to be able to say he was abusive. Something about divorce being wrong in the Bible." Paisley rolled her eyes. "They were so hypocritical."

Grabbing loosely onto her forearms, I let my hands slide down until they were gripping hers and pulled her into my chest. "Why didn't you ever tell me?"

"Because we moved away from him when my mom finally divorced him. She met my stepdad a year later and we moved here with him for his job a year after that. That's how I met you. By that time, I was mostly just bitter toward my mom for so many things. For making me grow up watching her entice him into beating her. For leaving me without a parent or two for the rest of the night. For teaching me when I was young that calling the cops would only harm the church." She snorted. "So by the time I met you, I was distancing myself from my mom, forgetting about my dad, and falling in love with a boy who had a calming effect on me that I'd never known was possible."

I shook my head, still not able to grasp all this. "I didn't even know he was your stepdad, I've met him . . . I've spent so much time with your parents."

"He's great, and he's great for my mom. She's changed a lot since she met my stepdad. But you didn't know because I felt closer to him than I did my real parents, and that's why he adopted me so I have his last name. My mom's nothing like she used to be, but I still don't like being around her. And that's why I don't like churches or cussing."

"Did he ever . . ." I trailed off, not able to voice the rest of my question.

"No, never! He never went looking for the fight; she just wouldn't stop until he did. But once the cussing stopped, he was done. And, obviously, I wasn't about to make him mad."

"I'm so sorry, Pay, I'll stop. I swear I—I'll try."

"Eli," she said on a laugh and tightened her arms around me. "Don't worry about it. Like I said, it *is* more of a joke between us now. Well, and Kristen too. It's not like I still associate those words with the person using them getting beaten up. I did when I was younger, and when we first met. But that was a long time ago; now I just don't find them necessary—unless you really make me mad for whatever reason." She winked.

"I don't know how you can joke about this."

"Because it stopped fourteen years ago." She shrugged like she hadn't just blown my mind . . . *again*. Like she hadn't just crushed this idea that my Paisley had grown up with the perfect life. "Drink," she ordered, and handed me my coffee.

"Yes, ma'am . . . ?"

Paisley bounced on her toes as she grabbed her empty coffee cup and the sandwich wrappers. "I can't kiss you until we're done with coffee and breakfast, and I really need to kiss you after that!"

I laughed loudly, took the lid off the cup, and leaned over to dump it in the sink. "All done."

Her eyebrows slammed down. "That's cheating."

"You'll get over it."

Grabbing around her waist, I hauled her small body back to mine and crushed my mouth to hers. One of her arms was caught between our bodies, her hand splayed against my chest, the other hand slowly trailed along my hair as her fingers curled around the back of my neck.

"Don't change because of that story," she begged. "Please just be the man I fell in love with."

"I can do that."

She smiled against my lips before kissing me once more. "Thank you."

Backing away from me, she grabbed all the trash and threw it away before moving out of the kitchen.

"Where are you going?"

"To brush my teeth and get dressed." She drew out the words, making them sound more like a question.

My eyebrows rose and I scoffed. "You're not getting dressed."

Paisley looked down at my shirt on her body before glancing up at me again. "Why not?"

"I'm nowhere near done with you yet, and your clothes will get in the way. I want you just like that for the rest of the day."

Her eyes widened and she bit down on her bottom lip. Letting her eyes trail down as much of my body as she could see from where I stood behind the counter, they bounced back up to my face before she took off running for my room.

I pulled off my shirt as I slowly followed behind—but my face fell when I realized her pile of clothes weren't next to my dresser, and the bathroom door was shut. Grabbing the knob, I glared at the door when it didn't turn.

"You better not put any more clothes on, Paisley."

She snorted, and I heard the water from the sink turn on.

As I reached above the frame, my frown deepened when I didn't feel the key up there. Looking around for something to jam into the small circular lock, I spotted the nightstand where Paisley always left a ton of her stuff. Right on top were hair pins that would fit perfectly.

Grabbing one, I widened it and shoved one of the ends

into the lock, unlocking and opening the door all in the same second.

Paisley straightened from washing her mouth in the sink, and I made a face before looking pointedly at the key sitting next to her on the counter.

"How'd you get it down?"

"I used my shirt to hit it," she answered with a defeated pout.

I nodded as I tossed the pin on the counter and went to stand behind her. She hadn't changed yet and was still only in my shirt. "Why are you running from me, Paisley?"

"Because I can?"

My eyes narrowed. "Do you not want me to touch you?" From the way her chest hitched with a harsh breath and her eyes became hooded, that wasn't it.

"I want to be able to touch you," she admitted in a soft voice.

I hardened instantly. "These weeks aren't about me," I reminded her.

"But—"

"I want you to, Paisley. You have no idea how much I want to feel you on me . . . but I want this for you so much more," I whispered against her neck.

Sliding my hands over her body, I let one move to her breast as the other ran past her hips to the inside of her thighs. Spreading them further apart, I slid my fingers over her entrance, trailing her wetness to her clit.

"Oh, Eli," she moaned, and arched her back against my chest.

"Hold on to me, Pay."

She wrapped her hands around the back of my neck and moved her hips against my hand.

"Open your eyes." Her dark eyes fluttered open, and I held them through the reflection in the mirror. "Look how beautiful you are."

Her cheeks were flushed, her eyes bright with desire, her full lips barely open as she breathed heavily. Her chest was pushed out against my hand where I was alternating between massaging one of her breasts and pulling gently on her nipple. Her legs were spread with my fingers moving in and out of her. And now her eyes were heating as she took in the sight.

I'd never seen anything more beautiful or perfect.

Pulling her bottom lip into her mouth, she bit down and stood on the balls of her feet as her body tightened, and I knew she was close. I rolled my fingers against her clit, and her eyes fluttered shut as her body started trembling.

"Open."

She forced them open, and her fingers dug into the back of my neck and she moaned as the trembling stopped for countless seconds before she fell apart.

I wrapped one arm around her waist when her knees gave out, but didn't stop touching her until her body sagged against mine.

When her eyes moved to meet mine in the reflection, all I could do was shake my head in amazement. "Beautiful," I murmured.

Mine. The girl in my arms was mine.

Chapter Nine

September 25, 2013

Paisley

"I CAN'T BELIEVE you're actually going to go through with this," Kristen said on a laugh that clearly showed how much of a mistake she thought this was.

"You're doing it with me."

"Oh no. No way." She pointed in the direction of the hallway leading to the rooms, and said, "There is no way in hell I am letting one of those ladies get anywhere near my vagina."

"Kristen!" I begged.

"You are making a huge mistake, I'm not about to make one with you."

My expression fell. "How is this a mistake? I need to do something, I've never . . ." I trailed off and gestured toward the area. "I've never taken that much care of it. I'm not about to have another weekend with Eli with a briar patch down there."

Kristen's sudden laugh was so loud that the receptionist jumped and looked over to us. "Is it really that bad?" she asked between her hysterics.

My lips twitched into a smile, and I admitted, "Okay, not *that* bad. It's somewhere between bush and jungle though. It needs help."

"I will be in there to support you and hold your hand, but you are out of your fucking mind if you think I'll be spreading my legs too."

"Language," I reminded her, and got an eye roll.

"You ready?" one of the workers asked as she and another uniformed woman walked toward us from the hall.

"Yep!" I said excitedly, and towed Kristen with me down the hall and into the room.

"You need two of them?" Kristen asked softly, but I didn't respond. It was all I could do to keep from laughing.

"Just remove everything below the waist, and we'll be back in a few minutes," the same woman said once we were inside.

Once she shut the door, Kristen was looking at me and pointing. "Why are there two table thingies?"

"Because you're doing this with me! I told you!"

"No I am not!"

"Kristen!" I complained.

"You are insane, Paisley! Eli won't even care if you have your fucking briar patch or nothing at all."

"Language," I muttered as she continued.

"There is literally not one thing that could make this kind of experience worth it. There will be no difference for you either way."

"How do you know? You've never done it before!" I reminded her.

"I don't care. I don't need to! I have enough of an imagination to know that it would be pointless."

"Just do it with me this once—"

"No."

"—and if I'm wrong, and there's no difference, I'll pay for a spa day for you."

Kristen eyed me for a second. "Three spa days."

"Two," I negotiated.

After another few moments, Kristen grabbed at her jeans and started unbuttoning them. "I am going to enjoy those two days, and I'll love them even more because you will have paid for them."

I laughed as I stripped down as well. Once I had everything placed off to the side and was hopping up onto the table, I looked back at my friend. "If I'm right and there's a difference after this, then you owe me."

Kristen snorted. "This pain will be payment enough." When she caught sight of my blank expression, she said, "Fine. What do you want, because I know you don't like going to the spa."

I thought for a moment, but nothing came to mind so I just shrugged. "Hundred dollars, and we'll call it even."

"That is so not even, you are getting the bad end of this, but deal!" After she was on her table, she pointed at me. "But you are only getting your money if there is a *good* difference from this."

"Fine."

Just then there was a short knock before the door slowly opened and the two women came back in. After they talked to us for a couple minutes, they had us lie back while they finished getting everything ready. And now that I was on a table with my legs spread in front of two strangers, I was regretting this. Why I never actually thought about the whole being-half-naked-in-front-of-strangers thing, I have no clue. My only thought had been that I'd wanted to do this so I wouldn't be mortified when Eli touched me again. If it weren't for forcing Kristen into this with me, I would have bailed.

"Oh my God! I'm sorry, I'll never ask you to do this again!" I screamed a few minutes later.

"Mother fucking son of a bitch, you bastard!"

"Langu—"

"Don't even think about *language*-ing me, you— *Mother fuck!*" Kristen yelled. "I hate you! I hate all of you in this roo— Oh my God!"

I was in so much pain while being completely amused by Kristen's yelling that I started giggling uncontrollably through my random bursts of cries and screams.

"Are you *laughing*?" Kristen shrieked. "Are you kidding me? You—ah! *Mother Russia!*"

The lady waxing me kept tapping the inside of my thigh to get me to stop laughing, but there was no stopping it now. The pain seemed to only fuel it. "Did you just—ow! Oh my God, ow! Did you just say 'Mother Russia'?"

"Shut up, Pay! I will never forgive yo— Son of a fuck!"

For fifteen minutes I laughed between my shocked cries of pain, and wasn't sure which one was responsible for the tears rolling down my cheeks; and Kristen continued swearing at everyone while telling me that we would never be friends again after this. When we were done and dressed again, Kristen wouldn't even look at me; she just kept mumbling that I owed her five spa days after what she'd had to endure.

"It burns," I complained when we were back in my car. "I feel like I can't close my legs."

I looked over and laughed when I found Kristen slumped down in the seat with her legs spread as far as the car would allow her. "Does yours burn?"

"Yes, Paisley! My vagina fucking burns!" She glared at me and snapped, "Don't even think about it!"

I pulled out of the parking lot and headed toward Kristen's house, but the entire time I wanted to hold my vaj like a little kid who needed to pee. "Maybe it won't be so bad the next time?" I offered.

"There will *not* be a next time," she said, appalled that I would even suggest it. "I will never again go along with *any* of your insane ideas. This one was the worst of all."

My mouth curved up, and a short laugh bubbled up my throat. "I still can't believe you yelled, 'Mother Russia' while we were in there."

"Shut up," Kristen mumbled, but her tone held a hint of humor. "I don't even know where that came from." When I pulled up in front of her house and didn't turn the car off, she looked at me in confusion. "Aren't you coming in?"

"I can't, I really feel like I need to go ice myself. It burns so bad."

Kristen laughed, but when she started moving out of the car, her laugh died and her face twisted in pain. "Ice sounds good."

"Let me know what Jason thinks!" I called out before she shut the door.

She turned to look at me, and once again she looked like she was ready to kill me. "You are out of your damn mind if you think I'm letting him anywhere near this tonight," she said as she pointed at her vaj. "See you on Friday, and I want more Eli details!"

I said my good-byes to her and waited until she was in her house before I put my car back into drive. My amused expression fell into a frown, and I cupped myself as if that would relieve the pain. "Ow," I mumbled pathetically to myself. "You're so stupid, Paisley."

"THIS IS ALMOST too weird for me," Kristen said two nights later, and I turned my head to look at her. She pointed back and forth between Eli and me. "Like, this will take forever to get used to."

Eli laughed against my shoulder and placed another kiss there. Pointing at the glass that had just been set on the bar in front of us, he asked, "Did you want to down it? It'll give me fair warning that you're pissed."

I made a face and moved his Guinness aside. "No thanks."

"So are you dating now?" Kristen asked. "Are you official, is there a title . . . ?"

Glancing at Eli, I shrugged and looked back to my friend. "We're just us," I said at the same time Eli declared, "She's mine."

Kristen and Jason both smiled. "Yours. Got it. Very official then," Kristen said with a wink.

Eli's knees tightened against my hips, and I leaned back into his chest. *Mine.* He'd been calling me that all week, and I couldn't get enough of it. Because we'd both been slammed with work, we'd only been able to see each other once this week—which wasn't a lot for us even before all this began.

He'd let me know earlier that he was coming to my place after O'Malley's tonight and wouldn't be leaving until Monday morning. There'd been so much promise of what was to come, but instead of waiting in heated anticipation for tonight . . . I had been dreading it. I'd gone and pretty much ruined any chance of enjoying or experiencing those promises on Wednesday night with Kristen. I'd been dying to know if she was sharing my unpleasant experience, but was too afraid to ask because if she hadn't, she would never let me live that night down.

I involuntarily crossed my legs together, and had to bite back a cry of unwelcome pain at the action. I sighed and wondered how I was ever going to get out of this weekend with Eli.

Kristen elbowed me and leaned in close. "So what did he think . . . ?" She raised an eyebrow and looked down, and I laughed awkwardly.

"I haven't seen him until we showed up here, but I really don't think he'll have much of an opinion," I grumbled lamely.

"Jason cared. I'm pretty sure Eli will too."

My eyes widened. Even though I was experiencing the most awkward pain of my life, I loved knowing that after how skeptical Kristen had been, there had been a difference. "Better or worse?"

"Better."

"Really?" I asked excitedly before remembering that it didn't matter for Eli and me anyway. The reminder made me so uncomfortable I didn't even want to tell Kristen that she owed me a hundred bucks.

"Oh yeah."

Eli pulled me back and nuzzled against my neck. "What are you two whispering about?"

"Wouldn't you like to know?" Kristen challenged. I *so* did not want him to know.

"Actua—"

I stumbled back into the bar stool when Eli's voice and body suddenly disappeared from behind me, and I turned at the same time Kristen gasped.

"Brett!" I screamed when he punched Eli in the face. "Brett, stop!"

Eli was lying on the ground, and Brett had a hand

gripping the back of his shirt, his other was still in a fist as he cocked back his arm to hit him again. Eli's hands moved quickly, one gripping Brett's forearm that was holding on to his shirt, the other to grab his fist that was aiming for Eli's face again.

Jason had run to pull Brett off, but stopped when Eli shoved Brett away and to the side.

Scrambling to his feet, Eli shoved his shoulder into Brett's stomach when he charged him again, sending them both into the wall we were sitting by.

"Stop!" I screamed, but Eli was only holding him there.

"I suggest you stop before I do something I regret," Eli warned.

"Why?" Brett growled. "After all these years, why now? You had her for *years*. Years, you bastard!" He tried moving out of Eli's hold, but Eli didn't budge. "Then I find her and she's finally living apart from *you*, and you have to come and decide that you want her now? You had your chance!"

"You got your hit in, but you won't be getting another." Eli said calmly, but his tone was dark and threatening. "I deserved that, I know, and I'm sorry for what I put both of you through."

Brett's chest heaved as his eyes narrowed on Eli.

"But understand this, she always has, and always will, belong to me."

Two security guards walked up behind Eli and he looked over his shoulder when they spoke. "Break it up or take it outside."

"It's over," Eli said calmly, and pushed off Brett to come stand in front of me.

Reaching behind his back with one arm, he brushed my stomach with his fingers—as if to make sure I was still there and not leaving. I gripped his fingers with both my hands, but kept my eyes on Brett as he walked toward the doors of the bar. Just before he went through them, he turned to look at me—the pain and sadness apparent on his face. My chest ached, but even through the pain I still had no doubt I'd made the right decision. Watching him walk away and leaving him last week was nothing compared to walking away from Eli.

It was like trying to compare a tidal wave to a ripple in a pond—it couldn't be done.

"Are you okay?" Eli asked. His palm slid across my cheek to hold my face in his hand.

Moving my eyes from the doorway to Eli's blue stare, I balked. "Me? Of course I'm okay, are— You're bleeding!" I reached for his face to wipe away the blood trickling out of the corner of his mouth, but he gripped my hands in his, stopping them.

"I'm fine. But, Paisley—"

"What even happened? You were there and then you weren't. By the time I turned around you were on the floor, how many times did he hit you?"

Eli pressed his forehead to mine, and immediately his calm demeanor flooded my veins. "Once, only once. He pulled me off the bar stool and I hit the floor. But I'm not worried about me right now."

"Of course you're not." I laughed shakily and rolled my eyes.

"That's the first time you've seen him since . . . ?" he asked, the question trailing off, but I knew when he was talking about.

"Yeah."

"Then I need to know if you're okay. I need to know what you're feeling right now, Paisley. After seeing him . . . after what just happened."

My gaze darted to the door before looking back into his stormy blue eyes. "Honestly?"

"Always."

"It hurt seeing him, but not as much as it would kill me to have you leave. I made the right choice, Eli. There's no questioning that." Pulling one of my hands free from his, I placed my hand over his jaw and brushed my thumb over the blood, wincing when his body jerked. "Sorry."

"He can punch, I'll give him that."

He wiped at his lip as he straightened, and looked down at the blood on his hand before rolling his eyes. Grabbing one of the bar napkins, he cleaned it off and picked up his Guinness. I made a face as he downed half the pint.

"That's disgusting." He grimaced and slammed the glass back down.

"As I've been telling you for years!"

Eli smirked and wrapped an arm around my waist, pulling me close as he bent down, and letting his lips fall onto mine. "The beer mixed with blood, Pay."

"Ew."

"Exactly." He kissed me again, and I pushed against his chest.

"You taste like nasty beer now," I whined.

"And you love it."

"Lie. That is such a lie."

He laughed and captured my mouth again, this time slowly teasing my tongue with his, and I melted into his arms and that kiss despite the Guinness aftertaste.

"Is it okay if I still don't know how to feel about all this?" Kristen asked. "I'm happy, and weirded out, and feel like I've stepped into an alternate universe . . . so many conflicting emotions."

Eli was smiling down at me when he pulled back, but he spoke to Kristen. "You have time to get used to it." Working his jaw a few times, he reached for his glass again and drained his beer. "Ready to get out of here?"

Grabbing his keys out of his pocket, he handed them to me and my eyes widened. "You're letting me drive your truck?" Not that I hadn't before. But it was always only because I'd won a bet, and I'm pretty sure I knocked five years off Eli's life every time I did.

"I don't know . . . can you reach the pedals?"

My expression fell and I smacked his stomach. "Don't be rude or I'll take your keys and leave you here."

He gripped my hips and pulled me closer. "It was an honest question. You're munchkin-sized."

"I am *not* a munchkin!"

Ignoring me, he lifted me into his arms and kissed me soundly. "Perfect pickup size."

"I'm leaving you here," I grumbled against his lips.

"I want to get out of here. I want to be alone with you, and I just got punched and chugged a pint all within the last five minutes. So, yes, I want you to drive."

I frowned and gently trailed my fingers over his red jaw. "'Kay, let's go, giant."

He snorted. "Troll."

"Take that back!" I demanded.

"The cute ones with the colorful hair that sticks straight up," he backpedaled.

"That does *not* make it any better!"

"It makes you adorable," he countered. He was still holding me, and turned so we could both see Kristen and Jason. "Later."

"Bye," they called out in unison, both smiling widely at us.

"Did you hear what he called me?" I asked as Eli began walking us away.

Eli kissed my forehead and squinted his eyes in concentration before smirking. "We could even give you the colorful hair and everything. Like I said, you'll be adorable."

People were whistling and shouting catcalls as Eli walked me out of the bar—if only they knew what was actually going on right now.

"Trolls are *not* adorable, you beast."

"Does that make you Beauty?" he teased.

I growled unimpressively. "This is not the time for you to try to be sweet."

"But you're pint-sized, you *are* adorable."

"And you look like Lurch."

He laughed loudly before everything stopped at once. Eli stopped walking, there was no sound coming from him, and even though we were out near the ocean air, it suddenly felt thick with tension . . . and I knew it was all coming from the man holding me.

"Paisley," he sneered my name, and my body froze. "Get back in the bar and stay with Kristen. Have Jason come out here."

"What's—"

Eli stopped my head from turning to look behind me as he let my body slide down his. "Please just go inside until I come get you."

I was looking up at Eli, but he was staring directly past me—his blue eyes were dark and his body was vibrating.

"Who's behind me?" I asked hesitantly.

"No one," he answered. When I tried pulling away, he looked directly into my eyes. "Please, Pay."

"Why can't I look? What is it?"

He took a large breath in before releasing it through his nose; his eyes never once left mine. "You'll see it later anyway, but right now I don't know *if* he's still here, and I will beat the shit out of him if I see him. And that is something I really don't want you to see. So, *please*, just trust me that going inside would be best right now."

Eli said *he*. At that moment, I could only think of one person who that might be. If what had gone on in the bar had barely fazed him, then I couldn't begin to imagine what Eli was looking at that was having this kind of effect on him. "If you honestly think Brett had something to do with whatever is behind me, then I *need* to see it even if he is still here, which I doubt he is after what just happened in the bar."

His arms didn't loosen, and the worry on his face seemed to multiply. His lips pressed into a firm line as he watched me, and he began shaking his head slowly.

"Don't try to protect me from this," I whispered my plea. "And don't make me leave you right now because I will go crazy in that bar wondering what is happening out here."

After a few more seconds of silence, Eli released me with a heavy sigh, only to loosely wrap an arm around my waist as he pulled his phone out of his pocket. I waited long enough to see him text Jason, then dial a nine and a one before I turned around, and my stomach sank.

All the windows on Eli's truck were smashed out, as were the windows on the cars on either side. But for those cars, it was only the windows that were directly next to Eli's truck.

He couldn't have. Brett wasn't vindictive like this. I knew he was hurting . . . but he wasn't violent. He wasn't this guy.

"I need police," Eli said calmly. "Yeah, I'm at O'Malley's on H Street, someone broke all the windows on my truck . . ."

I blocked out what he was saying as I tried to understand what was happening. As I turned around to see if any other cars looked like they'd had the same fate, the sinking feeling in my stomach only seemed to double when I didn't see anything else out of the ordinary.

Brett wouldn't do this, I told myself. But, then again, I wouldn't have thought that he would come looking for Eli to punch him either.

"That fucker," Jason sneered when he and Kristen joined up with us.

"Oh my God! How did no one see him do this?" Kristen asked.

Apparently everyone thought it was Brett.

Searching for my phone in my pocket, I tapped on the screen until it was calling Brett's number, but it went straight to voice mail.

"Of course," Eli gritted out, having heard. "How convenient."

A few police cars pulled up minutes later. Two officers began checking out the truck while another questioned Eli.

"Is there anyone you know of who might do this?" he asked a couple minutes in.

Eli eyed me warily and his grip on my waist tightened. "Her ex showed up tonight and tried to start a fight. Pulled me off the bar stool and punched me before I was able to stop him, security walked him out not even five minutes before we came out here. If it was him he would've had to have done it beforehand."

"Name?"

"Brett Oswell," I answered. "I tried calling him and his phone went straight to voice mail."

The officer nodded. "I'll need any information you have on him, ma'am."

"Of course."

We talked to the cop and security guards from the bar for thirty minutes before Eli pulled me in for a short kiss. "Go home with Kristen and Jason, and I'll come get you when all this is taken care of."

"No, I want to be here with you."

"And I want you safe while this is happening. After what happened with Rachel and my dad, I don't want you alone and I don't want you out here now that it's getting dark. I don't know Brett, but I know he's pissed and has already shown it in one way that we're positive of—that alone makes me want to keep you from him. If he did this?" he said, gesturing toward his truck. "I'm not leaving you alone ever again. My buddy who owns a window repair shop is on his way. By the time I come get you tonight, my truck will look like nothing happened. All right?"

I glanced over to Eli's truck and the two cars on either side, and my eyes drifted over the officers and owners of the other vehicles. "Okay," I conceded, and shook my head in disbelief.

Kissing me harder this time, he held me close to his chest as he spoke to Jason. "Keep my girl safe. Anything happens to her tonight—"

"I'm dead, I figured."

"Give me your phone, Pay." My eyebrows drew together as I handed it to him, and he placed his cell in my hand. "If Brett calls your phone, I'm answering. I'll call you when I'm coming to get you."

"See you soon," I whispered as I backed away with Kristen and Jason, but it sounded more like a plea.

If Brett had done this, I didn't want to be away from Eli at all. But I didn't want him to have to worry about me while trying to get things straightened out here. So with one last look, I turned and left.

Chapter Ten

September 27, 2013

Eli

I KNOCKED ON Jason's door a few hours later, and looked around at the dark street—trying to see anything that seemed off. I couldn't prove that Brett had been the one to vandalize the cars, but it would've been stupid for me to think for one second that it could've been anyone else. And while I knew it was just paranoia from what had happened with Dad and Rachel, I was afraid if I let my guard down for a second, something would happen to Paisley.

"Hey, so what all happened?" Jason asked before the door was even fully open.

I stepped in and looked around for the girls as I responded, "Got asked the same questions a few more times. I tried calling Brett twice but it still went to voice mail, but I heard two of the cops talking about cameras that were on the lights in the parking lot, so hopefully they find something. Where are the girls?"

He nodded his head in the direction of the bedroom. "Kristen's sitting with her on the bed . . . Paisley's kind of in shock about what happened. She kept saying on the way home that Brett wasn't an angry or violent guy. I think the fact that she was with someone who would do this is really getting to her."

I frowned as I crossed my arms over my chest. "I know she was falling hard for him, but she didn't know him long enough to know who he really was."

"I agree, and I think she's just come to that realization. How does the truck look?"

"Like nothing ever happened. We got all the glass vacuumed out and replaced, I'm just glad he didn't hit the frame." Looking down the hall, I took a step closer to Jason. "Do you think we shouldn't bring it up around her? I gave one of the detectives who showed up my number; told him to call me if he had any more questions about Brett. I don't want them calling Paisley about him, I don't want her to be brought into this anymore—especially if she's already not handling it well."

"Yeah, you're probably right. And if it ends up it *was*

him? That's going to be too hard for her. Do you know if they'll tell you if they find out who did it?"

"Once they get the video from the cameras on the lights and outside the bar, if they see the person doing it on there, they'll call me in to see if I can ID him." When Jason nodded, I took a step in the direction of the bedroom. "Thank you for bringing—"

"Don't thank me. I knew she needed to get out of there, and we would do anything for her."

Clapping his back, I sent him a grateful look. "Appreciate it, man. I'm gonna take her back to my place."

"You guys can stay in the guest room if you want," he offered. "I doubt it will take O'Malley's long to get the video over to the police, so if they do call you, they'd probably be doing it soon. You can stay here; that way if you need to leave she can be with us."

I hesitated for a few seconds as I thought about what to do. All I wanted was to take Paisley to my apartment and keep her safe, but I didn't know if Brett knew where I lived, and Jason had a point. "If you're sure?"

His expression fell. "You're both our best friends, you think I'm not going to try to help you out right now? Yes, I'm sure. Besides, Kristen already put new sheets on the bed in there just in case."

I nodded my appreciation. "Thank you."

Turning, I walked down the hall and into their bedroom. Paisley was lying on her side with her knees curled up to her chest and her head in Kristen's lap as Kristen ran her fingers through Paisley's long, dark hair. Kristen looked up at us and smiled, but Paisley didn't move until I ran my hand down her arm.

"Hey, beautiful."

Her head turned slowly; her dark eyes were wide. Her jaw was locked so tight it looked like she would break if she tried to speak.

"Let's get some sleep, all right?"

She nodded subtly, and I grabbed her up in my arms before turning to leave the room. Paisley never said anything about the fact that I wasn't taking her outside, or that I set her on her feet in Kristen and Jason's guest room . . . she just stood there staring at me with those wide eyes. Like she couldn't believe what had happened, and didn't know what to say now.

After shutting the bedroom door, I moved back to Paisley and slowly pulled her shirt off her body before unclasping her bra and letting it fall to the floor as well. Grabbing the back of my shirt, I lifted it over my head and off my arms, only to slide it over Paisley's head. When she was drowning in my shirt, I took off my jeans then grabbed for the button on her shorts. Letting them fall down her legs, I left her to step out of them while I went to arrange the pillows on the bed the way she liked them.

When they were all propped up, I slid under the covers and held my arm out for her. She came easily and curled up against my side as I wrapped my arm tight around her body, but she stayed rigid for long minutes until I pressed my lips to her forehead.

"Sleep, Pay," I crooned deeply.

The tension slowly left her body and her fingers curled

against my stomach as her head rested more comfortably on my shoulder. Her breathing deepened, and she was asleep within a few minutes.

"I've got you, and I love you."

MY EYES FLEW open the next morning when someone opened the bedroom door, but my body instantly relaxed when Jason walked in.

"Sorry," he whispered, and walked over to me with my phone. "Paisley left this in our room. Detective," he mouthed the last word.

Trying to clear my throat without waking up Paisley, I looked down at where she slept soundly on my chest, and turned my head away from her. "This is Eli Jenkins."

"Yes, this is Detective Hooper, we spoke last night in the parking lot of O'Malley's. Good news, the three vehicles were in sight of one of the cameras, and we have someone on video doing the vandalism. I was wondering if you'd be able to come down to look at what we have, see if you can ID the person."

"Of course, when do you need me?"

"As soon as you can get here."

"I'm on my way." After ending the call, I dropped my phone on the bed and looked back over to where Paisley's head rested on my chest, and pressed my lips gently to hers before sliding out from under her.

"Where you going?" she mumbled as I pulled my jeans on.

I wanted to keep all this from her, but I didn't want to

lie to her. I took in a deep breath as I thought of what to say to her, then decided to go with the truth. "I need to go to the police station to see if I can ID the person from the cameras at O'Malley's. I'll be back with breakfast soon."

"So they'll know if . . ." She trailed off. Her eyes, heavy from sleep, still told me everything she was feeling. Confusion, confliction, worry . . . but they were so distanced I doubt she saw me nod.

Walking over to the bed, I leaned over her and kissed her more firmly this time. "I love you, Pay."

Paisley wrapped a hand around the back of my neck to keep me there a few seconds after the kiss ended. She looked like she wanted to say something, but eventually released her hold on me, and said, "I love you too."

Just as I got to the door to leave the room, she called out my name to stop me. When I turned to look at her, she was sitting up and shaking her head. "I don't want to know if it was . . . I just don't want to know."

With a nod, I left the room and walked down the hall, and found Jason pouring coffee in the kitchen. "Do you have a shirt I could borrow?"

"Yep. There are travel mugs in the cupboard, get one."

I switched places with him when he left for his room, filled a mug with coffee, and finally located the matching lid by the time he came back out with a shirt.

"It's big on me, should fit you," he guessed as he tossed it toward me.

Shrugging into it, I grabbed the mug and turned toward him. What I was about to say must've been clear on my face because he leveled a glare at me.

"She'll be fine. Just go take care of whatever you have to do."

"Thank you."

"Stop thanking me."

I smirked as I walked past him. "Only if you let my girl get hurt."

"I still value my balls and my life."

Turning to look at him, I shrugged. "Then I'll keep thanking you."

I WASN'T AT the department long. It had still been light enough out when he took a bat to the windows, and thank God O'Malley's didn't have piece-of-shit security cameras, because there was no questioning who the guy was in the video.

I still just didn't understand how Brett could smash out all those windows in broad daylight in a crowded parking lot, and no one saw him. But, as the officers had told me the night before and then reminded me again while I was at the station, it happened a lot more often than people realized.

After picking up breakfast for everyone, I went back to Kristen and Jason's, determined to make Paisley have a good weekend. I'd told her about my dad and Rachel earlier this week, and then with this, I didn't want her focusing on all the bad shit. And if I was being honest with myself, *I* didn't want to keep focusing on all the bad shit. I knew with the first, their worries were now gone . . . but I didn't want last night to put a strain on us. I would make sure Paisley was safe, but I didn't want her worried about Brett doing something else. I didn't want her to keep wondering what bad could've happened later on down the road if she'd chosen him.

So as soon as I saw her, I dropped the breakfast on the table and pulled her into my arms as I walked her back to the guest room, my mouth never once leaving hers. This time, I didn't touch her. This time, it wasn't about anything sexual. This time was about telling her words I couldn't figure out how to form into sentences, with a kiss. This time was about showing her what she did to me and what she meant to me as I rested my body weight on top of hers on the bed. This time was about breathing the words "I love you" over and over as I trailed kisses across her neck to tease the sensitive spot behind her ear.

When I finally let us leave the bed to eat breakfast, Kristen and Jason both gave us looks like they'd known exactly what we'd been doing . . . but they had no idea.

I'd wanted to show Paisley what it felt like to have different experiences sexually since she'd never been given that attention before. I'd wanted to worship her body for these two weeks before I had sex with her. But I'd had no idea what just kissing her could do to us.

The passion that had filled the tiny room had followed us throughout the rest of the day. Touches were softer and lingered, looks lasted longer, and her smiles all hinted at a secret between us that no one would ever figure out.

And with every touch, with every look, and with every smile . . . I fell more in love with her.

September 28, 2013

Paisley

ELI AND I had started grossing out Kristen and Jason this afternoon with our "love fest," enough to the point where Eli had finally taken me out of their house. Even though he hadn't told me why he hadn't wanted to leave, I'd known. I knew he was trying to keep me somewhere where he thought Brett wouldn't find us, and that theory was proven once we'd left. After swinging by my apartment and telling me to pack a bag, he'd spent the day driving us up and down the beaches in Southern California, and going to all my favorite places along the way. We didn't get back to his apartment until close to 10 P.M., and while I'd been excited to get back since it had been such a long day, I was now wishing I was anywhere but here. Well, anywhere as long as I wasn't alone with Eli. Because Eli was now hovering over me and stealing my breath with teasing kisses and bites down my throat, and I just remembered that I desperately needed to avoid anything sexual with him.

"Did you have a good day?" I asked breathlessly, in hopes to get us talking instead of going in the direction we were already headed.

"I'd rather know if you did," he said against the spot behind my collarbone, then placed a deceptively soft kiss there.

"Of course I did. Thank you for everything. I loved everywhere we stopped, and—"

Eli cut off my rambling with a searing kiss that had my blood heating and my freaked-out mind clearing. The fingers that had been trailing up my arm began sliding down my body, caressing the swell of my breasts, and continuing their journey to my shorts.

No, no. No, no, no, no, no. I need to stop this. Now. Right now. Oh my God. This can't happen.

"Um!" I said loudly, and struggled to think of something. "How about we watch a movie?"

Eli laughed huskily. "Maybe tomorrow."

"Why not now? Don't you want to? Actually, I'm kind of tired," I lied, and swatted at the hand that was unzipping my shorts.

He abruptly stopped trying to undress me, and once again lifted his head to look at me. "Do you not want me to touch you?"

I would have shouted that I didn't if he hadn't looked absolutely terrified in that moment. I didn't have to ask what he'd meant by that question, it was all over his face and in the tone of his voice. He thought seeing Brett last night—or his actions—had put a wall between us. "Of course I do! Just . . . maybe not tonight. Or tomorrow," I added a few seconds after.

"Pay," he whispered in the same worried and hurt tone. "I will never touch you if ask me not to and mean it, but I need you to tell me what's happening right now."

"I'm just tired," I repeated, and immediately regretted the lie when Eli's face went completely blank.

"You're a bad liar, Paisley Morro, always have been."

He moved so he was sitting up and looking down at me. "What's really happening in that mind of yours? Is it . . . Are you—"

"No, Eli, no! I'm— God, I'm sorry. Please stop thinking whatever it is you're thinking; it has nothing to do with Brett." I covered my face with my hands and groaned. "This is so embarrassing."

"Embarrassing?" Eli echoed, his voice laced with confusion. A sharp laugh suddenly burst from his chest. "Are you . . . Is it that time of month for you, Pay?"

I dropped my hands and glared at him. "No, *Eli*, it's not. I just—" I cut off and groaned again. I knew my cheeks must have been bright red. "I tried to do something for you and it went *so so* wrong."

"Okay, now I'm really confused. Whatever it is, just tell me."

"This is so embarrassing! And you're going to laugh at me, and I just can't."

Eli lay back down beside me and brushed his fingers across my cheekbone. "If I promise not to laugh, will you tell me?"

I watched him for a few moments as I contemplated the outcome of this, and finally gave in with a sigh. "I thought it would have gone away by now." I bit down on my bottom lip and scrunched up my face. "I went and got waxed on Wednesday night, and I had a really bad reaction to it," I said in a rush and covered my face again so I wouldn't have to look at his anymore.

A hard laugh burst from Eli's chest after a few seconds of deafening silence. I felt the bed shift as he pushed himself up again and grabbed for my shorts. "I have to see this."

"No!" My hands flew to my shorts to keep them on my body. I'd thought I was mortified just telling him what was wrong; this was taking it to a whole new level.

"Pay, I *need* to see this, baby."

"You really don't."

"I'm pretty sure I do," he argued.

As much as I tried to keep him from taking off my shorts, Eli was stronger. And soon I was lying there with my hands over my face for the third time in just a handful of minutes. Eli was shaking the bed from how hard he was laughing. He dropped his forehead against my stomach and placed a few soft kisses there, and lightly brushed a finger across my overly sensitive vaj.

"Don't!" I yelled, and swatted at him.

"It's not that bad, Pay. I was expecting something *really* bad."

"Stop!" I said, and swatted once again. "It still hurts a little."

"How much worse was it?" he asked with an amused grin.

"So much worse. I almost didn't go into work on Thursday because of it."

His grin widened, and he brushed a finger across it again. "And it still hurts?"

"Yes, Eli!" I punched his shoulder as hard as I could, but he just started laughing again. "It still hurts, stop touching!"

"Okay, okay," he said on a laugh, and pulled my underwear back up, then my shorts. "I won't touch you until you're ready as long as you promise not to do this to yourself again."

"Deal," I agreed quickly.

Eli got up and walked over so he could grab my ankles and pull me off the bed. "Come on, let's go pick out a movie."

Chapter Eleven

October 2, 2013

Eli

"Switch," I said that next Wednesday, and held my cup in front of Paisley.

I hadn't. seen her since she'd left my apartment Monday morning—despite how much I'd begged her not to leave and even tried holding her down. At that point, I hadn't had an update on the Brett situation, and had no idea what would happen to her if I let her out of my sight. But the last three days had been quiet; and tonight there was no stress, and no worries. I couldn't help but notice how different everything felt from this weekend. Hell, even from two and three weeks ago.

My family was recovering from what had happened to my sister and dad. Brett had turned himself in; and while he probably wouldn't even face a year in prison, I doubted we would have problems with him again. And I had my Paisley. Every day with her was better than the last, and left me still wondering how it'd taken me so long to realize what I'd had right in front of me. But the past didn't matter anymore. I wouldn't waste another minute with her now that I had her, and I was never letting her go.

I'd been slammed at work all day and hadn't left until almost eight, but I'd needed to see Paisley. We went and grabbed a late dinner, and after staying there to relax and talk for a while, we'd driven out of town and were now at a secluded beach that had little crests overlooking the ocean. I'd backed up my truck on one of them, and we'd pulled the blankets out of the backseat to wrap ourselves up as we enjoyed the cool night air.

After we'd gotten milkshakes.

"There's nothing left in yours," she complained.

"That's why I said switch."

She laughed and jammed an elbow into my stomach. "Jerk."

When hers was empty as well, I set both cups down on the other side of the bed of my truck, and wrapped my arms around her waist to pull her close. We sat there for countless minutes just staring out at the darkened ocean, not speaking as I ran my fingers up and down her arms, across her stomach, and along her bare legs.

"What was that for?" I asked when a soft sigh came from her.

"I don't know. I'm just happy and calm. I love how it feels like no one can find us here . . . like we've found our own private place."

"I like the idea of having our own spot overlooking the ocean," I murmured, and let my hands glide up her stomach and over her breasts. Her lips parted and her breaths grew heavier as I focused on them. When a quiet whimper sounded in her throat, I slid my hands down to the top of her shorts, and quickly unbuttoned them and pulled down the zipper.

"Eli," she protested, her tone laced with anxiety.

My hands froze. "Is it still bad down there?"

"No, but—"

"Does it hurt?"

"No, it's fine now. But we're in public," she hissed.

I smiled against her neck and bit down teasingly in a way I was learning drove her crazy. "No one is out here, Pay," I said softly. "Remember what you were just saying." Sliding off her shorts and underwear, I slid my hand back up the inside of her thigh.

"But—oh God," she moaned, and my fingers stilled against her for a moment.

"Fuck, Paisley," I groaned against her skin.

"Language."

She arched off my chest when I pressed two fingers inside her and teased her entrance as I fought for control.

I'd never had a preference if a woman was bare or not, but something about the feel of Paisley, and knowing she did this for me, had me wanting to forget that I'd promised her another week before we had sex.

I pinched her clit, causing her to gasp and jerk back before pressing against my hand again, then gently massaged her. "Sit up," I whispered in her ear, and watched as goose bumps covered her arms and legs.

From the way she quickly turned to give me a confused look, she hadn't registered what I'd said until I was moving out from behind her. "Wait, where are you going?" When I knelt in front of her and began unwrapping the blanket, her eyes widened. "Eli, no. Not here."

"I think this is the perfect place," I disagreed. "And I've missed four days of this already." When she started protesting again, I leaned forward to press my lips against hers and teased her entrance with my hand. "No one can find us here. Remember that."

"I said it *felt* like it. If we found our way here, someone else could too!"

"No one's coming here, Paisley," I assured her, and lowered myself between her legs, staying just a breath away from her.

Paisley's eyes filled with heat, and her chest rose and fell sharply as she waited for what I would do. I kept my eyes on her the entire time as I slowly leaned forward to taste her, and her mouth fell open with a soundless huff when I flattened my tongue against her. She fell back so she was propped up on her elbows, and quiet moans and whimpers filled the night air as

I continued to tease her entrance with my fingers, and alternated with quick flicks of my tongue, and slow, hard strokes.

I watched as her head fell back and she tightened around my fingers, and when she barely started trembling, I sucked hard on her clit to push her over the edge and watched as her body fell apart. Paisley lowered herself onto the bed of the truck when it got to be too much, but I continued through until her body was only trembling from the aftershocks of her orgasm.

I moved out from between her legs and wrapped her up in the blanket before I sat up against my truck, and pulled her against me again. Looking over her flushed face and bright eyes, I smiled down at her. "Happy belated-Sunday."

She laughed shakily. "I can't believe we just did that out here."

"I told you, Pay, no one's here."

She tried to give me a stern look, but couldn't hold it. "And I told you, someone could've shown up."

"And they would've gotten one hell of a view."

"You're horrible." She laughed.

"I meant the ocean." I smirked when she elbowed my stomach. I ran my fingers over her sensitive bud, and my blood heated when her legs fell open and her eyes automatically shut, and a breathy whimper left her. "You think I'm going to let anyone else see you like that? This, these faces you make, and those sounds that come from you are for me, Paisley. No one else."

"No one," she agreed.

October 3, 2013

Paisley

MY EYES BLINKED open to a dark room, and I sat up quickly as I looked around for Eli. I was in his room, in his bed, but he wasn't there. I didn't even remember getting back in Eli's truck to drive home from the lookout point. Looking at the nightstand, I started leaning over to grab for his cell phone lying there when the sound of the running water registered in my mind, and my body relaxed.

Checking to see that it was a little after two in the morning, I scrambled out of his bed and into the bathroom. My eyes widened, and my stomach heated and curled in the most incredible way when I saw him standing under the spray of the shower with his hands running over his hair and the suds dripping down his body.

I knew I should go back to the bedroom, try to go back to sleep, or at least just wait for him to come in there—but even as I acknowledged those thoughts, I was slowly taking off my clothes and leaving them near the door.

Eli jerked back when I opened the door. "Jesus—Pay. . . . what are you doing?" he asked as his eyes ran over my body.

"Can I join you?"

He swallowed roughly, and his eyes darted up to my face and back my body. When he spoke again, his voice had dropped an octave. "I don't think that's a good idea."

"I know *you* don't think so, but I don't really care what you think right now."

Ignoring the way his voice conveyed his warning when he said my name, I stepped in under the hot spray, and finally allowed myself to look away from his face. Even with the nights over the last week and a half when he'd slept in his boxer briefs, I couldn't have been prepared for Eli like this. He was beautiful, masculine, and as I'd thought so many times before, built like a god. My fingers twitched as my eyes followed the lines from his chest, down his stomach, to that muscled V on his hips, to his erection.

I stepped forward and let my fingers run over his body, and my hands became bolder when a low groan sounded in his chest the lower I got; but just before I got to his muscled V, he grabbed my hands.

"If I let you go any lower, I'm not going to stop you from continuing, and you need to stop."

"Why, Eli?"

"I've told you, these two weeks are about only you."

"This is what I want," I argued.

Molding his mouth to mine, he growled "Not tonight" around the kiss as he pressed me against the wall.

"Not fair," I whimpered when his hand teased me and spread my legs. "Eli—"

"Your weeks, Paisley," he reminded me as he lowered himself to his knees, and lifted one of my legs over his shoulder.

"But you're just— Oh God," I moaned, and I wanted to punch him for knowing how to get his way.

My fingers gripped at the slippery, wet tile uselessly as his tongue reduced me to moans and needy sounds for the second time in just a couple hours. With only being on one leg, it was all I could do to stay standing as my body instantly responded to him.

The steam in the room, the constant spray from the shower, Eli's wet shoulders between my thighs, his fingers spreading me wider, and his tongue's assault had the tight knot in my stomach building faster than it ever had before.

The hand holding on to my back started lowering, and it wasn't until his finger was pushing against me that I even realized what he was doing.

"Please," I panted, and Eli chuckled darkly—the sound sending small shockwaves through my body.

His fingers continued until they took the place of his tongue, dipping inside me a few times before he trailed them back, circling around the place I was craving him— and yet didn't want him.

Just as slowly as the first time, Eli pushed one finger inside me as his tongue went back to licking and sucking me.

I cried out, and again wanted to get away from the intrusion, but at the same time my next plea for him to go deeper was on the tip of my tongue.

It no longer felt like there was a knot in my stomach. It felt like there was white-hot lava, and my entire body was vibrating in anticipation of what was coming—and just as it got closer, he would back off, making me groan in frustration until I was whimpering again.

It was the sweetest suffering I'd ever been through.

I came with a loud cry, and wasn't sure if I was still standing or had collapsed onto the floor. I wasn't sure of anything other than the pleasure and heat that were coursing through my body. I couldn't get enough of it . . . couldn't get enough of him.

My face scrunched together and a whimper bubbled up from my chest when he removed his finger. He gently set my foot back on the tile of the shower floor before standing to face me; the entire time he kept one hand on my waist like he was afraid I would fall. Which actually felt like a very real possibility right now.

Pulling me into his arms, he turned me so my back was against the spray, and reached to the side of me to grab the soap.

"You're perfect," he mumbled. "Absolutely perfect."

Unable to voice my thank-you to him, I nodded against his chest instead as I tried to control my breathing.

When he was done washing his hands, he ran the bar of soap over my shoulders and down my back. My body was exhausted from tonight, and while I should be tired from how late it was, my mind was extremely alert. And even though my arms and legs felt like they were weighted and useless, I forced my arms to move. Eli's erection was pressed firmly against my stomach, and best distraction ever, or not, I hadn't forgotten why I'd originally come in here. I still wanted this. I wanted to be able to touch him.

Bringing my hand between our bodies, I glided my fingers up his thick length, and Eli's body tightened as he hissed a curse.

"Paisley . . ."

Moving far enough away to allow what I wanted, I wrapped my fingers around his base and slowly stroked up.

"Fuck," he harshly whispered, and dropped his head back before looking down at me.

I sent him a slow, coy smile as I moved my hand down and back up, and his blue eyes became hooded as they looked down at where I was touching him.

His eyes shut for a few seconds before opening on me again when I added my other hand, and I nervously asked, "Like this?"

He nodded without saying anything, and brought one hand up to caress my cheek and brush back the wet hair hanging in my face. "Tighter," he said a few minutes later, and I gripped him harder in my hand.

A deep groan sounded in his throat before he slammed his mouth onto mine. Eli took advantage of my shocked gasp when he bit down on my bottom lip, and slid his tongue along mine. I could taste me and immediately recoiled, but Eli followed through with the kiss until I was greedily meeting the strokes of his tongue with my own.

The force of the kiss had moved us against the wall under the showerhead so the water was pouring down Eli's back as he bent over me.

"Fuck, Paisley, keep going," he begged with a rough voice, and pumped into my hand.

We both looked down to where my hands were moving from base to tip on his long length, and the only warning I had was the pause in Eli's rough breaths before he was coming on my stomach. He groaned with his release, and I just stood there staring as his hips slowed their movement. His chest moved roughly a few times before he bent and captured my lips again. This kiss was light, but searing, and moved through my body in a way I knew I would remember in the months to come.

"Let me wash you off," he breathed when he pulled away, bringing me with him.

Turning my body so my back was to his chest, he let the spray pound against my stomach as he reached for the soap he'd set down at some point, and rubbed it between his hands. I wiped at my stomach to get the lingering stickiness off me before he pulled me away from the water and began running his hands over my body.

He started with my shoulders and each arm, then moved to my chest and paid special attention to each breast before he moved over my stomach and hips, and around to my back. Kneeling down while he created more suds, he lathered up each leg before looking up at me with a wry smile and moving between my legs.

My body jerked, and I whimpered in protest. Everything was too sensitive after the last couple hours. "Too much."

His smile widened, and he stood and moved behind me to push me toward the water. "Guess I'll have to wait until we wake up."

A needy sound got caught in my throat, and he laughed softly.

When we finished cleaning, he wrapped me in a large towel before drying off his body and walking back into the bedroom. Not bothering with clothes, I crawled onto his bed and lay facedown, watching as he put on a pair of boxer briefs.

Grabbing a shirt out of the middle drawer, he walked over to me and pulled the towel away, ignoring when I whined and tried to hold on to it.

The whining stopped as soon as his lips touched the back of my right ankle.

With soft, openmouthed kisses and gentle hands, Eli made a line up my right leg as he came to kneel above me on the bed. I was squirming underneath him when he reached the back of my thigh, and even rose up on my knees in silent plea despite how I'd just asked him not to touch me again in the shower, but he continued up.

I felt him spread my bottom, and gasped. "Don't you dare, Eli Jenkins!"

He laughed and bit playfully on my butt before continuing to the small of my back and up my spine. By the time he reached the back of my neck, my entire body was covered in goose bumps, and I'd lost count of how many times I'd shivered.

"Put this on, Paisley," he said softly, and I blinked my eyes back open.

I pouted as I sat up on my knees; I hadn't been ready for that to end. Taking the shirt from his hand, I slid it over my head and watched him prop up the pillows on the bed. When he sat up against them, I looked at the spot by his side before moving onto his lap.

His blue eyes were playful, but held a hint of need. "So you liked sleeping like this, then?"

I bit down on my bottom lip when I felt him harden underneath me, and moved my hips against him.

I was right. Waxing was so worth it. It felt amazing.

"Paisley—"

"I want this, I want you. I don't want to wait until Sunday to be yours."

He smiled and sent me a puzzled look. "You are mine."

"I want to be *completely* yours, Eli."

Instead of immediately coming back with something about how these two weeks were about me, and once they were over we would . . . Eli sat there staring at me.

My eyes fluttered shut when I rocked against him again, and I had to bite back a moan elicited from the friction of the cotton on his briefs against me.

"God, you are the most amazing woman I've ever met, Paisley."

The truth in his confession stopped me from moving again, and I opened my eyes to find him staring at me in awe.

"You do things like this, and it is so hot. You're not afraid to tell me what you want, and you have no idea how much of a turn-on that is. The sounds and faces you make drive me crazy. And then you do something like ask for direction when we were in the shower . . . and the innocence in your question when you're doing something that mind-blowing just floors me.

"You're trusting me to do things and asking for things that make me want to do them for you over and over again. I love knowing I'm the one who's pushed you to try them. I love knowing you're experiencing all this with me. And throughout this sexy side of Paisley I'm meeting for the first time, I love that you're still my best friend. I love that you still give me shit. And my favorite thing in the world is when you look at me when I'm holding you, and I just know you're in love with me."

My lips tilted up in a smile, and I brushed my fingers along his jaw. "Eli . . ."

"I have this sweet, snarky, sexy girl, and I don't know what the hell I did to deserve her after how I treated her all those years." He pressed his lips softly to mine once before meeting my gaze again. "I want you, Paisley, so damn bad. But I wanted to give you these two weeks for a reason. I'm experiencing things for the first time just as you are, and I'm loving learning how your body responds to me first. It's just a few days, Pay, then I swear you won't be able to keep me away from you."

I laughed and my brow pinched together. "First time?" I had never planned on asking Eli about his past relationships, but his statement threw me off. "What are you experiencing for the first time?"

"Well, I never held anybody when I slept, as you already knew; that was always reserved for you. But having you sleep on top of me is definitely a first."

"Eli." I pushed on his chest to sit back to eye him suspiciously. "I've come over when girls were in your bed from the night before."

"If they didn't leave, they slept in the bed. But I never once held any of them. It seemed wrong—even then it was something I knew I only did with you." He pulled me back onto his chest. "Shower? Never been in a shower with anyone, unless I was a baby and don't remember."

"Really?" I was now starting to cheesy smile like a nerd, and I wouldn't have been able to stop it even if I tried.

He nodded and tilted my head back with his fingers to nip at my lips. "I've never tasted anyone before you just a few hours ago."

"That can't be true."

"It is. And this . . ." He trailed his fingers under the cheeks of my butt before sliding them up, teasing my tender hole. "Only you."

I gasped and my breathing deepened. "Then why would you . . . I don't understand. But you're good at these things."

"Porn," he answered my unfinished questions, unashamed. "Never wanted to try it on anyone until you. And the way you respond to it, Paisley? It takes everything in me not to make you mine right then."

I knew my face was red with heat, but I just sat there staring at him in shock. "All those are firsts?"

"Yeah, babe. So let's finish this last week of experiencing more firsts with you, and then I'm yours."

"Deal." I sat up to kiss him soundly. My face scrunched up in worry and embarrassment, and I quietly asked, "Will you spank me?"

His face fell and eyes widened. "What the hell . . . okay, I told you where I got my ideas, I want to know where *your* ideas have come from."

I shrugged and tried to sound as unashamed as he

had, but the embarrassment was still there in my tone. "Years of reading smut and dreaming about you."

A deep rumble came from his chest, and suddenly I was on my back and he was trying to pull the shirt off my body. A giggle burst from my lips from the quick change of positions and the way he was getting aggravated at the shirt.

"We're not going to sleep tonight."

I moaned when his teeth raked across my nipple, and gripped his hair in my hands. "Sounds perfect."

Paisley

ELI SMILED WIDELY at me when I walked into O'Malley's that next Friday. "Come here, beautiful."

I smiled against his kiss and felt myself relax in his calming embrace. I loved this man. I loved the way he made me feel. I loved how he—

"Your nine o'clock is from a long time ago, and she's been hinting hard for the last thirty minutes. Mind helping me out tonight?"

What? No, he wasn't about to do this to me again, this wasn't happening. My body locked up as hundreds of nights that had begun just like this one flooded my mind.

No, no, no, no, no! This isn't happening!

Eli sat back down on the bar stool and pulled me between his legs. His lips brushed against my neck as he whispered in my ear, "Christ, I thought you would never show up."

"Are you kidding me?" I gritted through clenched teeth, and pushed against the arms holding me close.

I felt his body tense and his lips pause against my neck for a few seconds before his eyes were directly in front of my own, but his hold never loosened. "What's wrong?"

"I have been your wingman for twelve years, Eli Jenkins. You're not about to keep treating me like one."

His eyes widened in confusion. "What are you talking about?"

"This, what you're doing right now? It's what you've always done. Use me as a shield from the exes and the crazies so you don't have to deal with them, and then push me back as soon as they're gone.

"Pay," Eli spoke up, the confusion in his eyes turning to amusement, but I kept talking over him.

"The words, the kisses against my neck, the way you're holding me . . . all of it. I'm not doing—"

My rant was cut off when Eli tipped me back against the bar and pressed his mouth firmly to mine. His large hands squeezed my waist then dropped down toward my hips when his tongue slowly slid against mine; and by the time he was nipping my bottom lip, I had forgotten we were still in the bar.

"Now if you'll let me speak," he murmured against my lips, then pressed another gentle kiss to them. "I'm sorry, all of that came out wrong in the beginning, that was my bad. I wanted your help in letting her know that I'm taken, not in just getting rid of her because I didn't want to have to deal with her again. But you're right, I shouldn't have said or done that." Eli sat back on the bar stool and pulled me close. His tone was low and serious, and his eyes were staring intently into mine. "You already know how sorry I am for everything I ever did to you and how I treated you before. I could apologize for that for the rest of my life, but it wouldn't help us move on from it. But I *am* sorry for tonight, I didn't mean to make you feel like a wingman again. Soon everyone will know that I belong to you. Soon we won't have to deal with these girls anymore, and I'm sorry that you have to now."

A shaky breath left me when he leaned forward and pressed his lips to the corner of my mouth, and my body slowly started relaxing again. "I may have overreacted . . . kinda," I mumbled lamely, earning a low laugh from him.

"Start over?" Eli offered.

My mouth curved into a smile, and I nodded against him. "Please."

In a move that had my head spinning, Eli turned to the side and pushed me a few feet away, only to pull me back so I slammed into his chest. "God, Pay, I've missed you," he growled against my mouth, and kissed me through my laughs.

"You're ridiculous," I murmured, and kissed him lightly once more. "But thank you."

With a wink, he got settled in his seat again and pulled me close. "So how was your day?" he asked, and reached for his Guinness.

"It was long, I was just ready to get here."

"A particular guy couldn't have something to do with that . . . could he?"

I raised an eyebrow and shrugged. "I don't know, is he a giant?"

Eli grinned. "A beast."

"Look kinda like Lurch?"

"Only after a night where his girlfriend wore him out."

Blood rushed to my cheeks and I looked around to see if anyone was paying attention to us.

"Speaking of," he murmured into my ear. "Are you trying to kill me with that outfit, Paisley? I'm not going to make it through the night if I have to look at you in this."

I frowned and looked down. I had a reason for wearing this; I just didn't think he'd like the actual outfit. I was in a loose black cotton skirt, and a dark gray shirt that hung off both shoulders but was extremely form-fitting around my waist and hips. Granted, the skirt was ungodly short, but, then again, so was I. This outfit was not sexy; I'd wear it hanging out with Kristen in a café.

"Uh . . ."

"Do you know how hard it is not to touch you when there's nothing stopping me?" Eli asked, and my breath came out in a rush. "Do you know how badly I want to take you into my truck right now to show you what I think of you wearing it?" He pulled me forward another inch and I tried to keep my expression neutral when I felt his erection on my stomach. "Do you realize I'm thinking of all the ways to make you moan when I get you back to my apartment tonight? And all the ways you're going to beg me not to stop once Sunday is here?"

If we even make it to Sunday, I thought to myself. I bit back a smile and pulled away enough so I could look at him. "Glad you're enjoying it."

"Tease."

"You have no idea."

His eyebrows shot up and his blue eyes took on a heat I was becoming familiar with. "That's it, we're leaving."

"Hey!" Kristen called out. "Sorry we're late."

I smiled mischievously at Eli when a defeated look crossed his face.

"Why don't I trust that face?" he asked.

"Probably because you shouldn't."

"What are we talking about?" Kristen asked as she sat down next to Eli.

I looked over at her and grinned widely. "Ways to drive Eli crazy until he gets me alone."

She had an oh-really expression on her face, and Jason looked like he'd swallowed something horrible. Conversations that had to do with anything remotely related to sex, he didn't want a part of. "Honeymooners," they both grumbled.

"Whenever you want to stop being adorable and pawing all over each other, let us know. The real world is ready for you to rejoin the cult of people who have normal lives."

"That sounds boring." Eli wrapped an arm around my waist and pulled me back since I'd been inching toward Kristen, and rested his chin on top of my head as he reached for his glass.

"You should go two weeks without sex," I blurted out, and Eli started choking on his beer.

Kristen rolled her eyes. "You mean two weeks without is uncommon?" she asked dryly.

Jason let his hand fall heavily to the bar and sighed. "I need a beer!"

Kristen fought a smile, but her shoulders shook from her silent laughter. I heard enough from her to know they weren't having problems in that department, but torturing Jason was too good an opportunity to pass.

"I mean two weeks where it's not *allowed*. See how hard it is."

Eli's hand tightened on my waist and he pulled me back against his erection again.

Kristen glanced behind her with a small smile on her face. "Two weeks actually sounds like heaven. A little mini-vacation from you, we should do it."

Jason's head jerked and he looked at the back of her head. "Seriously? Are we having this conversation right now? And pick one, either act like we always have it, or act like we don't."

"We should try it."

"We are not talking about this. We're in a fucking bar, for Christ's sake." Jason's neck and cheeks were bright red, and Kristen was no longer holding back her laughter.

"I want to be in the honeymoon stage again," she complained, and gestured toward Eli and me. "I want to be this annoying to people when we're out in public."

"You should totally do the two-week challenge," I chimed in. "Maybe even end it with a second honeymoon; it could be epic."

Jason glowered and pointed at Eli before pointing at me. "I blame you for this. What have you done to little innocent Paisley?"

Eli snorted. "Innocent."

A look of horror crossed Jason's face. "Don't say that to me! In my mind she's little innocent Paisley."

"Well, don't say that like I'm twelve or something," I huffed. "That just makes this creepy."

"Troll," Eli whispered.

"Chewbacca," I shot back.

"He spanks her," Kristen whined—puppy eyes and all.

"Wh-what?" Jason gave me a double take before he stopped looking at me altogether. "No, no."

"He does." I sent him an awkward smile when he chanced a look again and shrugged, and Eli bent down to whisper, "You told her about that?"

"We're girls," I explained. "It's what we do."

"I need that visual out of my head." Jason groaned.

"He—" Kristen began, but Jason cut her off.

"For the love of God, stop. I don't want to know what they do. This is *Paisley*."

"Yeah, I wouldn't want to know about Kristen," Eli muttered, and I elbowed him in the stomach. He must have gotten the hint to stop agreeing with Jason, because he added, "You should try it, man. Just sayin'."

Jason ran his hands over his face before grabbing Kristen's hand. "Fuck you both," he grumbled toward Eli and me, but he had a determined look on his face as he began towing his wife away from the bar.

"Have fun!" I called after them, and Kristen turned around, an excited smile lighting up her face.

"Shut the fuck up!" Jason groaned.

I laughed against Eli's chest and turned to face him.

"That would've been nice to have been clued in beforehand."

"You choking on your beer was priceless, though." Running my hands through his hair, I pulled his face closer to mine to kiss him softly. "I'm sure Jason will thank us later."

He laughed and shook his head. "I can't believe you told Kristen."

"Like I said, we're girls, it's what we do."

"If you say so." He rolled his eyes. "So back to you being a tease . . ."

My eyes popped open. "Oh! We need to leave!"

"What? Why?"

Schooling my expression, I turned to look at him after waving down the bartender. With one eyebrow raised, I said quietly, "Just trust me."

The heat was back in his eyes as he closed out the tab and towed us out to the parking lot. With a quick, searing kiss, he got me in my car and jogged across the lot to his truck. The entire way back to his apartment I was working to build up the courage for what I wanted to do.

It was my turn to control this.

Eli grabbed for my bag filled with clothes for the weekend and began walking toward his door, but I stopped him.

"Uh, no. I need that back."

He slowly handed it back to me with a puzzled look now on his rugged face.

"And I need you to go pack for the weekend, then meet me back in your truck."

"Okay . . . ?"

I nodded and took a deep breath in. Step one had been a lot easier than I'd thought it would be. "Okay."

He unlocked the doors for me to climb into his truck, and I threw my bag in the backseat as I waited for him. Less than five minutes later he was walking back out with a small gym bag in his hand. Tossing it in the back with mine, he climbed up front and cranked the engine.

"Now what?"

"Now . . . you drive south."

"How far south?"

"About an hour and a half if we're lucky. I'll let you know when we need to exit."

His eyes narrowed suspiciously, but he looked over his shoulder and backed out of the space without asking any more questions. My heart was racing as I waited for us to get on the freeway, and I had to grip my hands so I wouldn't continue to fidget with them. If Eli noticed my anxiousness, he didn't comment on it, and I tried to draw from his calm demeanor while simultaneously pumping myself up.

I could do this.

I could drive Eli crazy.

As soon as we were on the freeway and Eli wasn't changing a bunch of lanes anymore, I blew out a deep breath and raised my hips, bringing my hands under my short skirt to grab my underwear.

"What—holy shit," he breathed as I pulled them off and left them on the floorboard. "Pay, baby, what are you doing?"

"I had a reason for wearing this skirt, just not the one you were thinking." My voice shook as I turned in the seat and brought one foot up to rest on the dashboard, the other on the leather of the seat.

Eli's head quickly whipped back and forth between the freeway and where I was baring myself to him.

"You should focus on driving."

"Kinda fucking hard, Paisley," he gritted out.

"Language."

He looked back at me and bit down on his lip, but I'm pretty sure I still heard a curse in there. "Are you trying to get us killed?"

"No. Like I said, you really should focus on driving."

I sat there, completely exposed, and waited for almost twenty minutes before he finally relaxed his rigid frame and focused only on the freeway. Another couple minutes after that, I brought my hand down and ran my fingers along my wet lips; a gasp escaped my mouth when I did.

"You. Are. Not," he growled, and looked over at me.

His eyes widened before narrowing with what looked like anger. But I knew Eli enough to know that it was a frustration I was going to enjoy later. "Paisley."

I circled my clit before going lower to tease my entrance, and Eli's hands tightened on the steering wheel.

"I'm exiting the damn freeway."

"If you do, you can't touch me for the rest of the weekend. And I have this place through Sunday night. Jason talked with your boss, you have Monday off."

He wasn't looking at me, but his face fell as my words registered in his mind. "Evil. You are so evil."

Removing my hand, I waited for over thirty minutes before he calmed down again, and when he did, I went right back to where I'd been. I moved my hips against my hand, circled my clit roughly, and pressed my fingers inside me. Each moan, each whimper, each gasp had Eli clenching the steering wheel harder and harder.

By the third time I was playing my little game with him, he'd sunk down in his seat. He was gripping at his hair with one hand for a few seconds while he focused on driving before allowing himself to look again and whispering, "Fuck!"

My movements quickened, and Eli must have noticed the change in my breaths, because his warning came through the truck loud and clear. "If you get yourself off, I can make this go a lot longer than two weeks, Paisley."

I stopped abruptly. My breathing was ragged, and my body was aching for my climax.

"That's my job," he added. I started lowering my leg

from the dashboard, and he shot me a look. "Don't you dare."

Now I was the one glaring. I'd wanted to be in control. How had he turned this around on me?

"Not going how you planned?"

I didn't answer.

"Don't worry, Pay, your message wasn't missed. Just wait until we get to wherever you have us going."

Or maybe I *was* still in control. I smiled to myself and let my head fall back against the window as I waited for the rest of the drive to pass by.

I told him when to get off the freeway, and where to go, and he shot me a wide-eyed look when we pulled up to the Crystal Pier Hotel cottages.

"Pretty awesome, right?" I asked, and nodded my head in the direction of the dozens of cottages dotting the pier in front of us.

"How'd you pull this off?"

"I have connections."

Eli rolled his eyes, but smiled. "I'm sure you do." Turning off the car, he opened his door and stepped out. After getting our bags out of the backseat, he met me at the front of the truck and wrapped his arm around me. "Where do we check in?"

I took the keys out of my purse and dangled them in front of him. "Already done."

An amused smile played on his lips. "All right. Since you have this all planned out, lead the way."

We walked along the pier, passing people standing outside the cottages looking at the ocean, others sitting in chairs and drinking, everyone relaxed and enjoying the setting the beach provided. But thanks to the time of year and my friend who worked here, it wasn't full, and we had a cottage surrounded by empty cottages for the weekend.

Nothing but Eli, me, and the ocean . . . and no one too close to hear.

Eli was walking far enough away from me that our arms weren't even brushing together, and when I reached out to grab for his hand, he moved it away. I looked up with a confused expression that quickly fell as heat pooled low in my stomach from the look he was giving me.

His dark blue eyes held mine as we walked; the heat and want in them clear, but his face unreadable otherwise. Just before he looked ahead again, the corner of his mouth curved up in a smirk that had me stumbling.

I was so not in control of this.

Stopping in front of our cottage, I fumbled to get the key in the lock as Eli pressed up behind me, and I shut my eyes as I breathed out deeply, trying to compose myself.

"Need help?" he asked, a hint of enjoyment in his tone.

I didn't respond. Once I successfully had the door unlocked, I let us in and flipped on the lights before shutting the door behind Eli.

He set the bags down on the floor and turned to look at me, that same look he'd been giving me on the pier was back on his face. My heart skipped a beat before pounding painfully in my chest, and I backed up until I was against a wall—my legs and arms trembling with anticipation.

For countless minutes we just stood there staring at

each other, the tension in the room growing with each minute that passed. And while I was quickly losing the composure I'd been trying to build, Eli was still standing there like none of this was affecting him and he knew exactly what kind of effect it was having on me.

"You're trying to make it happen before Sunday," he guessed, and I sagged against the wall. He nodded, taking that as a confirmation, and held his arms out to his side. "You're running the show this weekend, come on, Pay."

"Wh-what?"

"You put on that show in my truck. You played with me that way to get *your* way. Come on, don't stop now; come have your way."

He continued to stand there with his arms out-stretched, and after the shock wore off, I slowly pushed off the wall and took small steps toward him. Looking up at his expectant gaze, I shakily reached out and lifted his shirt, and let him pull it the rest of the way off. Un-buckling the thick leather belt and sliding it out of the loops, I reached for the button and zipper on his jeans, and watched as they pooled at his feet.

With a smirk, he kicked off his shoes and stepped out of his jeans before standing in front of me again. "What now?"

I gaped at him for a few seconds. "Undress me." Even though I'd meant for it to come out demanding and erotic-sounding, it came across like a question.

And even though I was practically a statue through-out the entire thing, Eli gave little touches that left those places of my body feeling like they were on fire.

When I was standing completely naked in front of him, he raised one eyebrow. "Now?"

I glanced across the studio to where the bed was, and grabbing one of his hands, led him over to it. Pressing my fingers to his stomach, I pushed until he sat down, and took deep breaths—trying to summon the same courage I'd had in the truck. But it was gone. I didn't know what to do; I didn't know how to start this with him.

Moving to stand between his legs, I threaded my fingers through his hair and brought his mouth to mine. Eli curled his arms around my waist, but I pulled back and looked down at his lap.

"I'm g-going to, I want to sit on y-you," I stammered, and Eli fought a smile.

Oh my God, what is this? This is worse than my first make-out in junior high! And Eli is trying not to laugh. It's time to run away!

Eli scooted back and lifted me onto his lap; a teasing grin was on his face as he waited for what would come next. But I was frozen. I couldn't make myself kiss him, I couldn't enjoy the fact that I wasn't wearing anything and he was only in his boxer briefs. I was shaking. I'd made this so awkward.

Leaning close to my ear, he nipped at the lobe, and whispered huskily, "Now?"

A shiver ran up my spine, and he laughed darkly. Everything about his tone in that one word changed from the last time he'd said it, and everything in the room shifted. My breaths were no longer coming too fast because I was screwing everything up, they were spiking because the same tension that had filled the room when we'd first walked in was quickly engulfing us.

He lazily trailed one finger down my spine, and his blue eyes held mine. "What happened to the girl who would climb on my lap and tell me what she wanted?"

I didn't know what to say, my mouth opened but nothing came out for a few seconds. "I felt brave then."

"And now?"

"Not so much," I admitted breathily.

Eli flipped us so fast it made my head spin. Pinning me onto the bed, he pressed his lips to my neck and I moaned when he gently bit down on the soft skin there.

"That's because you're not getting your way during those times; you like the fight, Paisley." His lips moved in faint brushes along my throat, down my chest, and just when he came to the swell of my breasts, he moved back up. "Just like you like when I push you to try or do something even when you're not sure about it. Babe, you're a siren when I'm in control. You make it practically impossible to say no."

My lips trembled along with my body, and I arched my chest against him. I was aching to have him touch me.

"You tortured me by making me watch you touch yourself for almost two hours, but you want me to be in control of this, don't you? Just like when you asked me to spank you, Pay. *You* asked for it, but when it came down to it you asked me to stop, and what happened next?"

"Uh," I forced out between my heavy breaths.

"I stayed in control, and I did it again, and again; and

soon you were moaning and begging for it, and coming harder than you have before."

I whimpered and writhed beneath him when the tips of his fingers trailed down my stomach, stopping just above where I was craving him.

"Let me control this, let me be the one to know exactly what you need. Because while I know you like trying to take control, Paisley, I know you love that I never give it to you."

I nodded, and my next moan was quickly cut off when his mouth slammed down onto mine. His tongue moved against my own in perfect rhythm with his fingers inside me. The unsatisfied ache from the car ride flared as I approached my climax, but I wanted more. I wanted all of him.

"Please," I whimpered when Eli bent to pull one of my nipples into his mouth.

Grabbing the band of his boxer briefs, I pushed down and ignored the warning bite that only made me want this more. Using my feet, I moved the material down his legs, and gripped his erection in my hand.

"Give me you," I pleaded.

"There's my girl," he growled in approval, and released me to slide my body up to the middle of the bed.

Crawling between my legs, he bent to capture my lips again as he slowly ran his hand down my left leg to wrap it around his waist, before doing the same with the right. Reaching his hand between us, he rubbed his fingers against my clit as he pressed his cock against my lips, letting it slowly slide against me, teasing me. If this was how he was going to tease me, I regretted teasing him in the car. He was so close, and I was so close to being his, that I was ready to cry out in frustration because it still wasn't close enough.

I was about to beg again when he rolled his fingers against me, and a body-numbing heat exploded inside me. My moan turned into a shocked gasp laced with pain when Eli suddenly pushed inside me, and filled me over and over again as my orgasm continued. I'd wanted more of him, but I hadn't been prepared for this. My fingers dug into his back, and my legs tightened against his waist as I stretched around him.

Leaning on an elbow, he cupped my cheek in one of his hands as his eyes held mine, and his pace quickened. My lips parted and shook when he went even deeper, and I wasn't sure how much more I could take.

Eli kissed my trembling lips, and didn't move away to whisper, "I love you." Minutes later his body stilled for long seconds above mine, then began vibrating. "Mine," he breathed.

I looked up at his bright smile and leaned up to kiss him again. "Always."

Chapter Thirteen

October 5, 2013

Eli

I WOKE TO the sound of waves breaking against the pillars, light filtering in through the windows, and Paisley lying across my chest the next day. This was my heaven, and I wanted it every morning for the rest of my life.

Glancing at the clock on the far wall, I smiled and stretched when I read the time. Almost one in the afternoon. We'd passed out sometime around five this morning, and I'd been convinced I wouldn't wake up for a day. I teased Paisley about the things she liked and for being insatiable, but, honestly, she'd brought something out in me that I hadn't known was there. I couldn't get enough of her, I was always ready for more, and was ready to push the boundaries to see how far she would let us go . . . only to push them a little further.

It'd never been like this before, but more than that, there'd never been the connection that I have with her.

Kissing the top of her head, I slipped out from underneath her and walked into the bathroom to take a shower. I waited for the room to steam up before I stepped under the spray, and welcomed the hot water that pelted down on my tense and aching body as I cleaned up.

I turned when the glass door opened, and a smile tugged at my lips when a barely awake Paisley stepped into the shower with me. She sagged against my chest, and wrapped her arms loosely around my waist so she could just hang there. Turning us so I blocked the water from hitting her, I stood there holding her with one arm, and ran my other hand through her long hair and down her back.

"Morning, beautiful."

She tilted her head up so that her chin was resting on my chest, and smiled tenderly at me; her dark eyes had a dreamlike look to them.

"How do you feel?" I asked cautiously, and my body tightened in response when she grimaced.

"I hurt." Paisley slowly moved her body, as if testing out each place, but never removed her arms from my waist.

"I'm sorry," I murmured, and pressed my hand against her cheek.

I grew painfully hard against her stomach as images from last night flooded my mind. I'd pushed the boundaries, she'd kept begging, and I'd pushed harder. I knew she'd be sore this morning, but I hadn't stopped.

Like I'd told her last night. She was my siren. It was almost impossible to tell her no when she asked for something.

"Don't be sorry," she said so softly I almost didn't hear her above the water from the shower. She bit down on her too-full bottom lip, and brought her hand between our bodies to run her fingers slowly over my cock. "What do you want, Eli?" The want in her eyes and the hint in her question were impossible to miss, but I pulled back from her hand and kissed her soundly.

"I want to go get food for us while you finish taking your shower, and come back to find you still naked. I want to take care of you and be so gentle with you today," I whispered, and traced my hand down the curve of her ass. "I don't care that I only opened my eyes to you a month ago, I feel like I've been waiting to start the rest of my life with you for years. I don't want to keep going home to an apartment that you're not at. I want you to move in with me until my lease it up, and then I want to buy a house on the ocean so we can wake up like this every morning."

Paisley pulled away from my lips; her dark eyes were wide and bright, and matched the smile crossing her beautiful face.

Looking down, I brought my hand up to brush my

knuckles against her cheek. "I don't want another day away from you. *That's* what I want."

"I'm pretty sure that sounds perfect," she said breathlessly.

"Good." Kissing her softly, I whispered against her lips, "Enjoy your shower, I'll be back with food soon."

After drying off and finding my bag still sitting near the door, I dressed and headed out in search for food for us to eat now, and to easily make in the cottage over the next few days so we wouldn't have to leave again unless we wanted to. An hour later, I walked back into the cottage to find Paisley propped up against the pillows, dark hair in wild waves falling around her, asleep on the bed.

Last night had been *that* intense.

Putting most the food in the small fridge and leaving the rest out, I leaned my hip against the counter and folded my arms across my chest as I watched Paisley sleep. There were so many things I hadn't told her while we were in the shower that had been begging to be voiced, and those thoughts had only grown louder while I was out getting food. But standing there watching her, I didn't know how I was supposed to keep them in anymore despite how rushed they seemed.

I slipped off my shoes and walked quietly to the bed as I pulled off my clothes. Climbing onto the bed, I pressed my lips to hers before making a trail down, and felt her stir awake when I passed her breasts.

"Hey," she mumbled huskily, and lightly dragged her fingers through my hair. "Did you get food?"

"I did."

Her breaths became louder when my kisses hit her lower stomach, and after a few seconds, she decided, "It can wait."

Propping myself up on my elbows, I settled my body between her now-bent knees, and traced imaginary circles on her stomach. "You're not on birth control." It wasn't a question, but she still shook her head. "I didn't wear condoms last night."

The corners of her mouth tilted up for a second. "I know."

"And I didn't buy any when I was out just now."

Her eyebrows slanted down over her dark eyes, and she asked, "Why not?"

"Jason told me you were ready to get married and settle down. Was that true, or was he saying that because he was hoping it would make me realize what I could lose?"

"That's true," she answered, drawing out the words to sound like a question.

"I wasted a lot of time with you, Paisley, I don't see a reason to wait for anything with you."

One eyebrow lifted, and a sharp laugh burst from her chest. "Are you saying you want to knock me up, Eli Jenkins?"

"I'm saying I'm trying to start on everything I mapped out for you in the shower, and everything I wasn't sure how to say." I glanced down to where I was still tenderly touching her stomach before meeting her gaze again. "I want to have a family with you, and I want to marry you. I want to love you for the rest of my life, Paisley."

Her wide brown eyes slowly filled with tears, and a beautiful smile covered her face. A line of tears fell down her cheeks when she shook her head subtly. "Eli, it has only been one month since you realized you were in love with me. I have been dreaming of that future with you for years, but for you and for us, we need to wait. We can't just get married right now."

"Why?" I asked impatiently, and earned a light laugh from her as she gently ran her fingers through my hair.

"Because I want you to be sure that is something you—"

"I am sure," I said honestly, cutting her off. "I told you, Pay, I feel like I've been waiting for this for years."

"And *I* have," she reminded me. "If you asked me— and I mean *seriously* asked me—there is no way I would be able to say no to you, Eli. But I think you've felt like you've been waiting for this for years because when you realized how you felt, you were immediately faced with not being able to have me. Those first two weeks, you were scared you wouldn't get a future with me, and now it's only been two more weeks that we've even been together and you haven't had to worry about us. I want you to give it some time until the newness of us has passed before you decide that getting married to me is something you actually want."

I studied her face for silent moments, and watched as the small trail of tears continued to fall. I knew exactly how long it had been since she'd shown up at my door to tell me she'd chosen me. But I wasn't going to change my mind weeks, months, or years from now. When I started to tell her that, I stopped abruptly, and my eyes widened. "Paisley," I whispered. "Are you still afraid that I'm only with you because I don't want to lose my best friend?"

She shook her head quickly, and admitted, "I'm still afraid that I'm going to wake up tomorrow, and I'll be in my bedroom worrying that you'll have a girl in your bed when I come over for our Sunday morning, and all of this will have been a dream."

"That's not going to happen," I promised her. "I'm going to make sure you wake up every morning for the rest of your life knowing exactly how much I love you." With a reluctant nod, I said, "If you really want to, we can wait another month to get married."

Paisley laughed softly and tugged at my hair. "A year."

"Fuck no."

"Language," she chastised. "A year," she repeated.

"And if I got down on one knee right now and asked you to marry me?"

"I would set the date for a year from now."

I groaned and dropped my head on her stomach. "When I thought about this conversation, it went a lot differently in my head."

"Oh yeah?" she asked teasingly.

"I thought you were going to have me drive us to Vegas today," I admitted against her skin, but still didn't look up at her.

Paisley was quiet for a couple minutes. She just continued to run her fingers through my hair, and just when I looked up to see her expression, she said, "People just wouldn't understand. They wouldn't know our story even if they know us, and they just wouldn't get it. I'm pretty sure Kristen and Jason wouldn't even agree with us doing everything so soon."

"Who cares about anyone else? I don't give a fuck what other people would think. I care about what *you* think, and what I want with you."

"But they would all give us their opinions. They would constantly be telling us how stupid we were, and they probably wouldn't show up to our wedding."

My face fell. "You don't even want a big wedding, Pay. And *again*, who cares about anyone else?"

Her eyes widened and her hands stopped moving. "How do you know I don't want a big wedding?"

"Because you've said that at every one of our friends' weddings."

"You remember that?"

My brow pinched together. "Of course I do. Just because I wasn't catching on to what you were waiting for from me, doesn't mean I wasn't listening to you."

She watched me in awe for a few seconds, then said, "I'm still not marrying you until a year is up."

I exhaled heavily and nodded. "I can wait a year to marry you as long as you'll still move in with me."

"As soon as my lease is up in four months."

"No. That is definitely too long."

Paisley laughed softly. "We can do a week at my apartment, then a week at yours, and continue doing that until my lease is up."

"Better," I agreed, then mumbled, "Does this mean I need to go back out and buy condoms?"

"Maybe you should have just gotten them your first time out," she suggested, and I sighed in defeat.

"Okay. I'll be—" I cut off when Paisley grabbed my arm and pulled me back down onto her when I'd started getting up.

"I'm kidding. I brought some with me; they're in my bag. I just wasn't really thinking about them last night or this morning until you brought them up."

I placed a kiss on her nose and got up from the bed to grab her bag. "You can't blame me if you get pregnant from last night."

"I doubt I got pregnant last night." She laughed softly. "But, oh my God, I can see your mom's reaction now if we got pregnant before we got married."

"Then I guess it would be Vegas or the courthouse for us," I grumbled like it would be a hardship to marry her.

Paisley just rolled her eyes. "I may not have ever talked to your mom as your girlfriend, but she's always known how I felt about you, and I know for a fact that she would kill us if we didn't have a huge wedding."

I was no longer surprised by anyone else knowing; I knew I'd been the only one blind to Paisley's feelings. "Did you ever tell her that wasn't what you wanted?"

"No . . ."

"Then who cares what she wants."

Paisley choked out a laugh. "Eli! She's your mom. You're supposed to care, just like I do."

I crawled back onto the bed with her and held her stare. "Tell me *exactly* what you want when I finally force you into marrying me."

Her eyebrows rose. "Force me, huh? Thanks for the fair warning," she teased, but then the humor in her eyes and smile changed into something softer. "I just want you. I don't want anything big, I just want simple. I want to wear a white dress, and I don't want to have to be around a bunch of people after. I just want it to be you and me, like we are right now. I don't want a ring—"

"Fuck that," I balked. "I'm getting you a ring."

"Language, and I don't want one! You told me to tell you exactly what I wanted, and I'm telling you."

"If you don't let me get you a ring, how are people supposed to know you're mine, Pay?"

When she spoke again, her voice was nearly inaudible. "I've always been yours, Eli. My love for you has never been a show for everyone else. It's always been just for you; that's not changing now."

Well fuck. She just had to go and put it like that. "No ring," I conceded with a sigh.

"If you want, I'll get a tattoo."

"You hate needles."

She shrugged and smiled mischievously. "I'll get a portrait of Lurch on my shoulder or something."

I dropped my head onto her chest, and my shoulders and back shook from the laugh I was trying to hold back. Once I was sure I could keep a straight face, I looked back up to her. "If you get Lurch, I'm getting a troll with purple hair."

Her eyes widened and her head shook slowly back and forth. "No," she mouthed. "But, that's what I want. I just want simple; I just want us."

"Then that's what it will be," I assured her. "Anything you want, Paisley. Always."

Epilogue

October 4, 2014 . . . one year later

Eli

"YOU'RE FUCKING KIDDING me."

"Language!" Paisley hissed. "And whatever it is, I doubt I'm kidding."

I walked through the cottage and into the bathroom where Paisley had just stepped out of the shower, and held up the box in my hands. "*Condoms?* Pay, you are out of your damn mind if you think I'm wearing condoms anymore."

She held out an arm like she had no idea why I was getting mad, but laughed when I was done. "It's a habit to make sure I have them since *someone* conveniently forgets to buys them *or* throws them away when he finds my stash."

"Is it so bad that I want to be able to look at you walking around with a big pregnant stomach?"

A small laugh burst from her chest, and she walked forward to wrap her arms around my neck. "It was because we weren't married. Your mom is already mad enough at me for having a small ceremony and nothing else. The last thing I needed was her giving me the same lecture she gave your sister when Kash informed everyone *right* after the wedding that Rachel was pregnant with twins."

My face fell. "Do we really have to talk about that right now? I'm still not okay knowing that my sister has had sex; you don't have to make it worse by reminding me that she's pregnant."

"Fine, we'll act like she got pregnant all by herself. No sex involved."

My eyebrows pinched together, and just as I started to tell Paisley how much that didn't make sense, I huffed. "Huh. Yeah, I like that actually. But none of that matters right now. What matters is that you're my wife as of four hours ago, I'm not wearing condoms anymore."

"You don't have to," she crooned, and kissed me softly. "Like I said, it was habit."

"I'm burning these," I grumbled against her lips.

"Fine." She leaned back enough to unwrap the towel, and let it fall to the floor. Grabbing my pants, she unbuttoned them and pulled the zipper down, then pushed them off me. Once she had my boxer briefs down past my hips and was gripping me in her small hands, she said, "But do you mind waiting until after? After all, like you said, it's been a whole four hours, and we still haven't made this marriage legitimate yet."

I grabbed her up in my arms, and covered her mouth with my own as I turned to walk her into the bedroom. "I fucking love you, Pay."

"Language," she mumbled halfheartedly, but soon the only sounds coming from her were incoherent words and erotic noises.

Four months after our first weekend here at the Crystal Pier Hotel, Paisley's lease ended and we *officially* moved in together. An entire two days before we announced our engagement—as our parents had been reminding us up until today. While our original plan had been to only have Kristen and Jason as our witnesses today, not one person in my family, or Paisley's parents, had been okay with that or allowed it to happen. And even though my mom had tried planning a "surprise reception" that wouldn't have exactly been a surprise, I'd finally gotten her to agree to stop pushing the reception issue about a month ago. Paisley didn't want one and refused to let me tell my mom because she didn't want to upset her more, but I'd promised Paisley she would have the wedding she wanted, and I wasn't going back on my word.

Even though it had been a joke between Paisley and me for the last year, we didn't get married at a court-house. We had a pastor marry us on *our* crest overlooking the ocean, and like Paisley had wanted, there were no rings, only two small tattoos that we'd gotten done right after the short ceremony. Paisley now had an outline of a small heart on the side of her wrist that went with the arrow I'd gotten on the side of mine.

And after a couple hours on the road, we were back in the exact same cottage we'd been in a year ago. There was no one in the surrounding cottages, no one would be able to get ahold of us for the next week, and there was nothing for us to do but spend every day wrapped up in each other as we started our life together that was long overdue.

THE END

Coming soon, the must-read book
for all Molly McAdams' fans!

Trusting Liam

A Taking Chances and Forgiving Lies Novel

When Kennedy Ryan moves to California, she
never expects to come face-to-face with Liam
Taylor—the intriguing man she hasn't been
able to forget. Somehow Liam managed to get
Kennedy to let down her guard for a single
night of passion that ended up meaning more
than it was ever supposed to. Accustomed to
disastrous experiences with men, Kennedy
shields herself before he can break down
more of the carefully built control she's clung
to for the last four years. But every time she
sees Liam, she feels her resolve weakening.

Liam Taylor has been asked to befriend
his boss's nieces. But what starts out as a
reluctant favor ends up leading Liam to
the only girl who ever slipped away before
morning—a girl he thought he'd never find

again. And now that she's within reach, Liam's determined never to let her go.

When a secret from her past tests their relationship, will they be able to cling to the trust Liam has worked so hard to build?

Available June 2015

Prologue

May 15

Kennedy

CRACKING AN EYE open, I immediately shut it against the harsh light coming into the room and bit back a groan as I felt the pounding in my head. Making another attempt—this time with both eyes—I squinted at the unfamiliar hotel room and blinked a few times, then let my eyes open all the way as I took in my surroundings. Well, as much of them as I could without moving.

There was a heavy arm draped uncomfortably over my waist, a forehead pressed to the back of my head, a nose to the back of my neck, and an erection to my butt.

What. The. Hell. I was naked; he was naked. *Why are we naked, and who is behind me?* If I wasn't seconds from screaming for someone to help me, I might have snorted. The *why* was obvious, there was a familiar ache between my legs, and my lips felt puffy from kissing and where he'd bitten down on them.

I inhaled softly. *He. Him.* Oh God.

Flashes from last night took turns assaulting me with the pounding in my head. Impromptu trip to Vegas with the girls after finals ended. Dancing. Club. Drinks. Arctic-blue eyes captivating me. More drinks and dancing. *Him* holding me close, and not close enough. Lips against mine. Stumbling into a room. Hands searching. *His* tall, hard body pressing mine against the bed—still not close enough.

My eyes immediately went to my left hand, and I exhaled slowly in relief when I didn't find a ring there. *Thank God, the last thing I need is a marriage as result of a drunken night in Vegas.* I rolled my eyes. The last thing I needed was a man in my life, period. And if my family didn't kill me for it, I would have died from embarrassment if I had ended up with a ring on my finger after last night. Because unlike what everyone loves to believe so they can feel better about their own dirty deeds while in Sin City, what happens in Vegas doesn't always stay in Vegas.

Trying not to wake him, I slowly slid out from under his arm and off the bed to search for my clothes. Once I was dressed, I told myself to just leave, but I couldn't help it—I turned to look at him in the light. I needed to be sure I hadn't made *him* up.

The images from last night tore through my mind again when I saw the large, tattooed arm resting where my body had just been. The muscles were well defined, even when he was relaxed, and the face had a boyish charm now that *he* was asleep. Such a difference from the predatory stare and knowing smirk I kept seeing in my mind. Before I could stop myself, I gently ran my fingers through his dirty-blond hair that, now in the sunlight, I could see had a red tint to it. And I knew if he opened them, those arctic-blue eyes would once again captivate me.

But I couldn't risk that.

I'd already stayed too long; I'd already made a mistake with him. Drunken one-night stands weren't my thing. Drunken one-night stands with strangers in Vegas were even worse.

Straightening, I turned and walked quietly from the room.

Chapter One

May 21 . . . One year later

Kennedy

"WHY ARE YOU trying to doing this to me?" Kira yelled as she stood from where she'd been sitting on the couch.

I looked over at my identical twin to see a look of horror on her face, and waited for the freak-out that I knew was only seconds away. Shifting my attention back to our parents, I mumbled, "Told you it wouldn't go over well."

"But—you can't—Kennedy, why—Zane's in Florida," Kira sputtered out, and I rolled my eyes at the same time as my dad.

"Is that supposed to mean something to me?" Dad asked as he crossed his large tattooed arms over his chest.

Not willing to give Kira time to respond to that kind of question, I started talking over Dad before he could finish. "Did you ever think that maybe a little distance might be a good thing for the two of you? And did you *not* hear Dad? These guys are out of prison, Kira!" I shouted, punctuating the last few words in case she'd missed the memo the first time around.

"Maybe Zane will go with you," Mom offered with a sympathetic look on her face that I knew was as well practiced as it was a lie. The worry was still there in her eyes, as was the eagerness to get us away from Florida . . . and it wasn't exactly a secret that we all wanted Kira to get space from Zane.

They'd been together since we were fifteen, and the more time went on, the more Kira's world revolved around only him. It was annoying.

"And leave his job?" Kira countered.

"Well, then maybe this will be good for you, like Kennedy said. Get a break from Zane so you can see other options. You girls are only twenty-two, you just graduated from college, and you're too young to be getting serious anyway, Kira, just ask Kennedy. You'll regret not enjoying life first."

"Wow, thanks for that, Mom. What's that supposed to mean?"

Before she could respond to me, my dad's head jerked

back and he sent Mom a look. "What the hell *is* that supposed to mean? You were twenty-one when we got engaged."

"Do I look like I'm not enjoying life suddenly? What did I miss?" I asked Kira as Dad spoke, but she didn't make any indication that she'd even heard me.

"Seriously, Kash?" Mom shot Dad a look that even I was impressed by. "That was different. *We* were different. She's *only* dated Zane."

"Can we get back to the more important discussion?" I cut in before Dad could respond, and looked back to Kira. "*I'm* going to California. *You're* going with me. *Zane* can deal with it."

"You can't do this! I'm not going!" Kira shrieked as the tears started.

"You act like I'm giving either of you a choice. Both of you need to start accepting this."

My eyes widened at my dad's dark tone, and I shot right back, "You act like you still have a say in our lives. You haven't for four years. And if you remember, I'm going along with what you want without complaint. So don't throw me into the same category as Kira when she's the only one fighting you on this."

One dark eyebrow rose, and I saw Kira sink back onto the couch from the look he was giving. Too bad I was just like him: hardheaded and stubborn. I might be my sister's mirror image, but I was nothing like her. I raised one eyebrow back at him, and Mom sighed.

"I don't know how I put up with you two sometimes,"

she groaned, rubbing her hand over her forehead. Looking at Kira, she said, "You're going to California, no more discussion. This is for your safety, why can't you see that?"

"I'm not going!" Kira sobbed. "Who cares if some guys Dad put away *years* ago are out of prison?"

I snorted, but before I could respond, Uncle Mason's deep voice sounded directly behind us. "These men do."

I turned quickly to look at him, and tried not to laugh when he gave Dad a questioning look and mouthed, "Zane?" as he gestured to Kira.

"Is there any other reason she would be freaking out like this?" I asked as I stood to go give him a hug.

"Are you both packed?" he asked.

"Packed?" Kira yelled again. "They just told us! I haven't even called Zane!"

"Oh my God, no one cares."

"Kennedy," Mom chastised, but I knew she was thinking the same thing.

As soon as Kira was out of the room, I sighed and headed to my room to pack as much as I could. Kira was already packing and sobbing into her phone when I passed her room, and I somehow managed to hold back an eye roll. Never mind that our parents had just told us that our family was being threatened by members of a gang our dad and uncle Mason had put away over twenty years ago. A gang whose members had kidnapped our mom before we were born and held her for over a month in an attempt to free their main members from prison. Or that a chunk of them were getting out of prison within the next handful of months. Or that Kira and I were the main targets of their threats. Nope . . . none of that mattered to Kira right now. What mattered was that we were going to be living in California for the time being—close to our mom's side of the family—and Zane wouldn't be going with us. No Zane meant devastation in Kira's world. She couldn't even get dressed without telling everyone about a memory with Zane in that outfit, or that it was one of his many favorites.

Snatching a hair band off my desk, I pulled my thick, black hair into a messy bun on the top of my head and started packing. I didn't turn to face Kira when she came into my room ten minutes later, but I knew she was there.

"How could you do this to me?" she asked quietly, her words breaking with emotion. "You're supposed to be on my side, you're *always* supposed to be on my side. And you went behind my back and planned this with Mom and Dad without even warning me?"

I glanced over my shoulder, my eyebrows rising at her assumption. "I didn't plan shit, Kira. They told me while you were talking to Zane right before they asked you to get off the phone. They just wanted me to know because they thought you would freak out and they needed me to be able to try to talk you into it calmly—rather than hitting us both with the news at the same time. The only difference between you and me is I have no problem with this move because I'm not stupid enough to think that the gang won't actually make good on their threats if we stay here. Or try to."

I went back to packing, and there was a couple minutes of silence before she said, "I know why you're all really doing this. Don't think for a second that I'm stupid enough not to realize this is about Zane."

I released a heavy breath and shook my head. "Despite what you think, this has nothing to do with you and your boyfriend. But I *do* think that this is something we need to do, and I think it will be good for us."

"I won't forgive you for this. You of all people should realize how much this is going to kill me."

My breath caught, but I didn't reply. I knew I couldn't without lashing out at her. Without another word, she left my room. The only sounds were her soft cries and her feet on the hardwood as she walked away.

"So NOW THAT you have us on a private jet—which just makes this all the more weird, by the way—do you mind telling us details about where we'll be spending the next however long?" I asked Uncle Mason a few hours later.

"Didn't your mom and dad tell you everything?"

I gave him a look that he immediately laughed at.

"Okay, tell me what you know, and I'll fill in the blanks."

"Basically, all I know is that Juarez and a handful of others from his crew are up for probation within a few months of each other starting next week. They're somehow threatening us—but more specifically, Kira and me—and Mom and Dad think it would be best if we weren't near Tampa. Since we just graduated and don't have a reason to stay up in Tallahassee anymore, the only other place to go is California, near Mom's family, and we'll be there for an undetermined amount of time."

"I wasn't told most of that," Kira muttered from where she was sulking across the aisle.

"You *were* told that," I shot back. "All of that. You just couldn't get past the California-equals-no-Zane part, and flipped while they told you the rest!"

Before we could start on another war, Uncle Mason spoke up. "You'll be just north of San Diego, near your uncle Eli. He's already been looking into places for you to live, and your parents are working something out with them for a car."

"Lovely. Sounds like everyone is already completely filled in," Kira sneered.

Uncle Mason didn't respond for a long time, he just sat there staring at Kira with a somber expression. It was so unlike him. "I don't want you two to have to do this any more than you do, trust me. Your dad and I know better than anyone what it's like to pick up and move at a moment's notice and not be able to have a say in it, so we know what you're going through."

Kira mumbled something too low for me to hear, but it was obvious in her expression that she didn't agree with him.

After a subtle shake of my head, I looked back at Uncle Mason and tapped his leg with my foot to get his attention again. "Okay, so we've heard about Juarez's gang and what happened with Mom being taken. But here's what I don't understand and am having a little bit of trouble with. Why, after so much time has passed, do you think it's them threatening us? Wouldn't they be over it by now? I mean, couldn't it just as easily be someone you've arrested recently, and you're just jumping ahead and thinking it's Juarez?"

Uncle Mason was shaking his head before I even finished asking my questions. "No. It may have been twenty-three years ago, but we haven't forgotten what happened, and we know for a fact they haven't and are still holding a grudge, because there have been letters delivered to your dad."

"What did they say?"

"It doesn't matter."

"What did they say?" I asked louder, and Kira leaned toward us in her seat to hear his response.

"I said it doesn't—"

"We deserve to know!" I snapped.

After a beat of silence, he admitted, "They said, 'Can't wait to meet the rest of your family,' or 'How are those daughters of yours?' " Uncle Mason sighed heavily and looked out the window for a few seconds.

"That's it?" I asked when he didn't continue. "I mean, that's really creepy but it doesn't prove much of anything."

"It does, because at the bottom it had the gang's symbol. A symbol your dad and I used to have tattooed on us when we were undercover. A symbol they left spray-painted on your parents' wall after kidnapping your mom."

"Oh," I breathed, and Uncle Mason sent me a look.

"Yeah. 'Oh.' "

May 27

Liam

Squeezing Cecily's waist once, I deepened the kiss for a few seconds before pulling away. A smirk crossed my face when she tried to follow me. "I gotta go."

"Just a little longer?" she asked huskily as she pulled on my tie, bringing us closer together.

"I can't. You know I have to get to that meeting." Grabbing her slender wrist in my hand, I took my tie from her firm grip and sent her a look.

"Of course, the so-called meeting that no one else in the office seems to know about." Her full lips pouted, and I exhaled slowly at the annoying look.

"You know about it."

Cecily smacked my arm and huffed. "Only because you told me."

"That's not my problem. Besides, it might be a bad thing that I'm the only one. Who knows? You may get your wish, I might be getting fired."

She smiled wryly and wrapped her arms around my neck before pressing her mouth to mine. "Now, that definitely sounds like a meeting I want to happen," she murmured against my lips.

"Power-hungry bitch," I growled, and kissed her hard once more before backing away.

"Man-whore."

"Hasn't stopped you."

Her gaze raked over me as I backed toward the door before snapping up to my face. "No, it hasn't."

I grinned and nodded in her direction. "Are you going to leave my office?"

She slid off the desk and walked around to sit in my chair. "I don't know, maybe I'll sit in here awhile to get used to what my new office feels like."

"I haven't gotten fired yet." Not bothering to wait, I walked out of my office and left Cecily in there. I looked behind me to watch the door shut as I fixed my tie, a soft smile tugging at my lips as I thought about the girl in there.

There was no bullshit when it came to Cecily and me. I didn't like relationships, labels, or being tied down to any one girl; and she liked guys who demanded control. It was the complete opposite of who she was, but I wasn't going to question it. She wasn't shy about her need to be at the top of everything—including a company—nor was she shy about her willingness to step on any and everyone to get there.

She wanted my job, I'd known that before we started sleeping together, but she couldn't have it. And despite our current status and her greed-filled eyes, she wasn't one to sleep her way to the top—we just happened to be a nice distraction for each other at work.

I looked up just in time to stop myself from running into the man standing in the hallway. He hadn't been moving; he was just standing there with his arms crossed over his chest, one eyebrow raised as he studied me.

"Excuse me," I said, and moved to walk around him—

he moved with me. My eyebrows slanted down, and I looked up at him. Yeah. Up. I was six-two. To have to look up at someone was saying something. "Can I help you?" I asked when I noticed his mirrored movement hadn't been a mistake; he was still staring down at me with a calculating expression.

The man didn't move, and he didn't say anything. With a huff, I gave him a once-over and smirked. My dad owned a boxing gym, meaning I'd grown up around some of the leanest, deadliest fighters around, as well as some of the biggest meatheads. But this fucker was massive. "If you don't mind, I have somewhere to be. And lay off the steroids, old man."

When I went to move around him this time, he let me pass; but when I looked over my shoulder, he was turned around and glaring at me with that same expression before he glanced behind him toward my office.

My footsteps faltered and I racked my brain trying to think of any mention of another guy Cecily might be seeing—one who would come looking for her at work—but I came up with nothing. And somehow I knew in the way he was glaring at me again that he wasn't looking at me like he was ready to fight. He looked like he was frustrated with what he was seeing in me.

Shaking my head as if to clear it, I looked ahead of me and continued down the halls to my boss's office. Before I got there, I stopped at his secretary's desk. "Hey, call security. There's a guy in here I've never seen before, and I don't think he's supposed to be here. Height is probably six-five. Weight is around two-seventy or two-eighty. The guy is solid muscle, tan, Caucasian, black hair." I watched as she jotted everything down. "Got it?"

"Yeah," she said as she grabbed the phone, but I didn't wait to hear the conversation.

Walking toward the office beside her, I knocked on the door as I opened it, and flashed a smile at my boss, Eli Jenkins.

"Hey, Liam, come in and have a seat."

I sat in one of the two chairs on the other side of his desk, and waited for whatever he had to say as he sat directly next to me. Despite what I'd told Cecily, I wasn't worried about losing my job. I knew Eli liked me and my work, and I was on the same path he'd taken in this industry. But that didn't mean he didn't know about Cecily and me, and our interoffice relationship wasn't exactly allowed.

Before he could say anything else, his eyes snapped up when the door to his office quickly opened.

"Two hundred and seventy to two hundred and eighty pounds? Hardly."

I turned quickly at the deep voice, and my eyes widened at the roided-out guy from the hall.

"Two hundred eighty-five, actually. I'm proud of those extra five pounds."

"Who the fuck are you?" I asked, standing up from the chair. Turning to look at Eli, I pointed at the guy. "I had security called on him."

"He called me 'old man,' can you believe that?" The guy snorted. "At least you were right about the height.

Good one, kid." He walked around to sit in Eli's desk chair, and I looked back and forth between him and where Eli was sitting next to me.

Eli rolled his eyes. "Liam Taylor, it's not exactly a pleasure to introduce you, but this is Mason Gates. He's a close friend of my sister and her husband."

"You *still* don't like me?" Mason asked Eli. "It was twenty-three years ago."

Eli shot him a hard look. "She's my sister. No, I still don't like you." Glancing over to me, Eli explained, "He also dated my other sister."

Mason snorted a laugh at the word "dated," but didn't say anything else to piss off Eli. Nodding in my direction, he said, "He's good. Probably dumb as shit, but he's funny, and he was pretty spot-on about me. Minus the steroids."

"I'm lost," I whispered to the room, and then looked at Mason. "What was your deal in the hall?"

"I already knew I wasn't going to like you. Any other questions?"

"Mason," Eli barked, then looked at me. "Act like he's not here. For whatever reason, he felt the need to be here when I talked with you."

"Okay . . ." I said, drawing out the word. "Talk to me about what?"

"Mason just brought my nieces to California from Florida so they could get away from a situation going on back home, and they're not exactly happy about being here. They know they need to be here, and that's all that's keeping them from going back to Florida, but they need something to do to keep them busy. A job, friends . . . anything. And I was hoping that you would be able to help with that."

I waited to see if he would add anything, and when he didn't, I shrugged. "I—sure. I mean, I don't know how much I can do to help them find friends, but if they're old enough for the gym, I know my dad is looking for a few people."

Mason cleared his throat, and Eli gave him an annoyed look before saying, "We also need to make sure that one of them, Kira, doesn't try to run back home. She has a boyfriend and is taking the separation harder than her sister. My sister and brother-in-law trust my judgment to find someone who can do that. I trust you as much as I trust my own son, and I think you and your connections will be exactly what they need to settle in here."

I laughed hesitantly and looked at both of them for a few seconds. "Are you serious? I'm not a babysitter, Eli; we work in advertising. Besides that, I'm twenty-four, what do you expect me to do with these girls that will make it seem okay for me to even act like their friend?"

"I knew I didn't like him," Mason blurted out, and stood. "Meeting over."

"Sit down," Eli ordered, but didn't look to make sure he did. "Liam, my nieces just turned twenty-two, they're close to your age. And no one is asking you to babysit them."

"You want me to make sure one of them doesn't run

back to her boyfriend! That sounds like babysitting," I argued.

"Still don't like him," Mason chimed in, but Eli and I didn't bother responding to him.

"I don't need you to watch her every move, I was just hoping that you could maybe include them in whatever you and your friends are doing one or two times over the weekends. See if the girls get along with you or your friends, try to get them to have a good time so they won't focus on how much they don't want to be here. You don't have to give up your life for them, Liam. And if you aren't willing to do that, and if your dad does have space at the gym for them, that would be more than enough. I won't ask you for anything else." When I just sat there staring at him, Eli leaned closer. "Please. I'd have my son do this, but you know he's backpacking through Europe this summer with his friends."

If it had been something as simple as inviting his nieces to a party, I would've done it in a heartbeat. But with Mason there—whatever his real reasons—and with the part that still sounded like I'd be babysitting them, I knew there was something else behind this than the girls just needing to be introduced to a few people. The fact that there was a "situation" back in Florida, and that they didn't want to be here, only confirmed that thought. But Eli was my mentor. I'd interned for him in college, and he'd hired me on after the internship had ended. He'd continued helping me throughout the last couple years of college, always pushing me to work harder and be better, and then did the same so I would work my way up in his company after I'd graduated. He'd done more than I could've ever asked for, and this was the first thing he'd asked of me. No matter how odd it seemed, I knew I couldn't tell him no.

"Okay," I finally agreed. "I'll call my dad. I know for a fact that he needs new people for the drink station in the gym. I'll see if he can interview them and let you know when."

"Perfect," Eli said on a relieved sigh. "They've already been here a week, I know they need to get out of their condo."

I nodded and reluctantly said, "And I'll make sure whichever one you mentioned won't go running back to her boyfriend. I'm sure a bunch of us will end up at the beach this weekend, at least. I'll let you know when I do."

"Still don't like him," Mason said again. "I vote we find someone else."

I rolled my eyes and looked over at him. "Why did you even need to be here?"

"A question I've already asked a few times," Eli mumbled.

Mason's teasing tone and expression quickly disappeared, leaving him looking at me the exact way he had been in the hallway. "I'm here because someone needs to tell you that you aren't to touch either of them. Rachel and Kash may trust Eli's choice in *you* being the one to help them out; that doesn't mean I do. No one chose you so you would have another girl to fuck."

"Mason," Eli snapped, but Mason's gaze never left me.

One eyebrow rose, and a short laugh burst from my chest. "Excuse me?"

"You didn't try to hide the girl who was in your office earlier, and that already makes me not like you as much as I could. You see an opportunity in a girl, and you take it. Trust me, I get it. I was the same way when I was your age, which is why Eli still hates me. But those girls mean the world to Eli, to me, and to their parents. This is me warning you now: If you touch one of those girls, you will have all three of us on you. And their dad is the last person you want to piss off. Your job is to be their friend. Nothing more."

"Noted," I huffed as I stood to leave the office. "Anything else, Eli?"

He shook his head at Mason, and sighed when he looked back at me. "Just remind Cecily that I don't want her in your office."

The corner of my mouth tilted up and I nodded as I turned to leave. "I'll call my dad and let you know what he says."

"I appreciate it, Liam. Really," he called out as I reached the door.

Mason snorted. "Still don't like him."

The feeling was mutual.

Immerse Yourself in the World of Molly McAdams

Taking Chances

Her first year away is turning out to be nearly perfect, but one weekend of giving in to heated passion will change everything

Eighteen-year-old Harper has grown up under the thumb of her career marine father. Ready to live life her own way and to experience things she's only ever heard of from the jarheads in her father's unit, she's on her way to college at San Diego State University.

Thanks to her new roommate, Harper is introduced to a world of parties, gorgeous guys, family, and emotions. She finds herself being torn in two as she quickly falls in love with both her new boyfriend, Brandon, and her roommate's brother, Chase. Despite their dangerous looks and histories, both men adore Harper and would do anything for her, including taking a step back if it would mean she'd be happy.

Immerse Yourself in the World
of Molly McAdams

Taking Chances

Her first year away is turning out to be
nearly perfect, but one weekend of giving in
to heated passion will change everything

Eighteen-year-old Harper has grown up under
the thumb of her career marine father. Ready
to live life her own way and to experience
things she's only ever heard of from the
jarheads in her father's unit, she's on her way
to college at San Diego State University.

Thanks to her new roommate, Harper is
introduced to a world of parties, gorgeous guys,
family, and emotions. She finds herself being
torn in two as she quickly falls in love with both
her new boyfriend, Brandon, and her roommate's
brother, Chase. Despite their dangerous looks
and histories, both men adore Harper and
would do anything for her, including taking
a step back if it would mean she'd be happy.

when disaster sends her running into Tyler's
arms, Cassi will have to decide whether
to face the dangers of her past . . . or to
burn her chance at a future with Gage.

From Ashes

Aside from her dad, who passed away when
she was six, Cassidy Jameson has only ever
trusted one man: her best friend, Tyler. So
of course she follows him to Texas when he
leaves for college. She just didn't expect to
be so drawn to their new roommate, Gage, a
gorgeous guy with a husky Southern drawl.
The only problem? He's Tyler's cousin.

Gage Carson was excited to share an apartment
off campus with his cousin. He didn't mind
that Tyler was bringing the mysterious
friend he'd heard about since they were kids
. . . until the most beautiful girl he's ever
seen jumps out of his cousin's Jeep. There's
something about Cassi that makes Gage want
to give her everything. Too bad Tyler has
warned him that she's strictly off-limits.

Despite everything keeping them apart,
Cassi and Gage dance dangerously close to
the touch they've both been craving. But

when disaster sends her running into Tyler's arms, Cassi will have to decide whether to face the demons of her past . . . or to burn her chance at a future with Gage.

step back from the girl who has become
his whole world. If it means she's happy?

times will be pressed. Friendships will be put
to the test, and hearts will be shattered.

Stealing Harper

A *Taking Chances* Novella

Chase Grayson has never been interested in having a relationship that lasts longer than it takes for him and his date to get dressed again. But then he stumbles into a gray-eyed girl whose innocence pours off her, and everything changes. From the minute Harper opens her mouth to let him know just how much he disgusts her, he's hooked.

But a princess deserves a Prince Charming who can make her dreams come true. Not a guy who can turn her life into a nightmare.

All good intentions go out the window when Harper starts to fall for the guy Chase has come to view as a brother. He wanted to protect her by keeping her away, but he can't stand to see her with anyone else, and he'll do anything to make her his. But when it comes down to Harper choosing between the two, will Chase have the strength to

**step back from the girl who has become
his whole world if it means she's happy?**

**Lines will be crossed. Friendships will be put
to the test. And hearts will be shattered.**

Forgiving Lies

A matter of secrets . . .

Undercover cop Logan "Kash" Ryan can't afford a distraction like his new neighbor Rachel Masters, even if she's the most beautiful woman he's ever seen. To catch a serial killer, he needs to stay focused, yet all he can think about is the feisty, long-legged coed whose guarded nature intrigues him.

A matter of lies . . .

Deceived and hurt before, Rachel would rather be a single, crazy cat lady than trust another guy, especially a gorgeous, tattooed bad boy with a Harley, like Kash. But when his liquid-steel eyes meet hers, it takes all of Rachel's willpower to stop herself from exploring his hot body with her own.

A matter of love . . .

As much as they try to keep it platonic, the friction between them sparks an irresistible heat that soon consumes them. Can Kash keep Rachel's heart and her life safe even as he risks his own? Will she be able to forgive his lies . . . or will she run when she discovers the dangerous truth?

Needing Her

A *From Ashes* Novella

She's the Girl Next Door

Maci Price isn't really into relationships.
Having four very protective older brothers
has always made having a boyfriend very
difficult anyway. But her friend is set on
finding her the right guy—and thinks the
mysterious Connor Green is the perfect pick.

He's Her Brother's Best Friend

Connor Green is trying to find himself
again. He loved, then lost, and it's time for
him to pick up the pieces. His brooding is
making his friends crazy, but Maci, who has
grown up into a gorgeous and incredibly
sexy woman, is about to break the spell.

They're Made for Each Other

When Maci starts up old pranks to get Connor out of his slump, an all-out war leads to a night that will break all their rules . . . and a relationship they must keep hidden. Together they're electric. Apart they're safe. And soon they'll each find that they're exactly what the other needs.

gagie to keep her safe. When his time as
Rachel's protector runs out, Trent will turn
his back on the man he's known—and risk
everything if it means getting her out alive.

Deceiving Lies

A *Forgiving Lies* Novel

Rachel is supposed to be planning her wedding
to Kash, the love of her life. After the crazy year
they've had, she's ready to settle down and live
a completely normal life. Well, as normal as it
can be. But there's something else waiting—
something threatening to tear them apart.

Kash is ready for it all with Rachel, especially
if "all" includes having a football team of
babies with his future wife. In his line of
work, Kash knows how short life can be
and doesn't want to waste another minute
of their life together. But now his past as
an undercover narcotics agent has come
back to haunt him . . . and it's the girl
he loves who's caught in the middle.

Trent Cruz's orders are clear: take the girl. But
there's something about this girl that has him
changing the rules and playing a dangerous

**game to keep her safe. When his time as
Rachel's protector runs out, Trent will turn
his back on the only life he's known—and risk
everything if it means getting her out alive.**

Capturing Peace

A *Sharing You* Prequel Novella

Coen Steele has spent the last five years serving his country. Now that he's back, he's finally ready to leave behind the chaos of the battlefield and pursue his lifelong dream. What he wasn't expecting was the feisty sister of one of his battle buddies— who has made it obvious that she wants nothing to do with him—to intrigue him in a way no woman has before.

Reagan Hudson's life changed in the blink of an eye six years ago when she found out she was pregnant and on her own. Since then, Reagan has vowed never to let another man into her life so that no one can walk out on her, or her son, again. But the more she runs into her brother's hot and mysterious friend, the more he sparks something in her that she promised herself she wouldn't feel again.

Can two people with everything to lose allow themselves to finally capture the love they both deserve?

stolen moments and nights that end too soon.
But is their love strong enough to bear the
weight of Kamryn. Is Brody strong
enough to confront the pain of the past and

Sharing You

Twenty-three-year-old Kamryn Cunningham
has left behind a privileged, turbulent past
for the anonymity of small-town life. Busy
with her new bakery, she isn't interested in
hook-ups or fix-ups. Then she meets the very
sexy, very married Brody. Though she can't
deny the pull between them, Kamryn isn't
a cheater and she's not good at sharing.

Twenty-six-year-old Brody Saco may be
married, but he isn't happy. When his
girlfriend got pregnant six years ago, he did
the right thing . . . and he's been paying for
it ever since. Now, his marriage is nothing
but a trap filled with hate, manipulation,
and blame—the remnants of a tragedy that
happened five years earlier. While he's never
broken his vows, he can't stop the flood of
emotion that meeting Kamryn unlocks.

Brought together by an intense heat that is
impossible to resist, Brody and Kamryn share

stolen moments and nights that end too soon. But is their love strong enough to bear the weight of Kamryn's guilt? And is Brody strong enough to confront the pain of the past and finally break free of his conniving wife?

Letting Go

A Thatch Novel

Grey and Ben fell in love at thirteen and believed they'd be together forever. But three days before their wedding, the twenty-year-old groom-to-be suddenly died from an unknown heart condition, destroying his would-be bride's world. If it hadn't been for their best friend, Jagger, Grey never would have made it through those last two years to graduation. He's the only one who understands her pain, the only one who knows what it's like to force yourself to keep moving when your dreams are shattered. Jagger swears he'll always be there for her, but no one has ever been able to hold on to him. He's not the kind of guy to settle down.

It's true that no one has ever been able to keep Jagger—because he's only ever belonged to Grey. While everyone else worries over Grey's fragility, he's the only one who sees her strength. Yet as much as he wants Grey, he knows her heart will always be with Ben. Still they can't deny the heat that is growing between them—a passion that soon becomes too hot to handle. But admitting their feelings for each other means they've got to face the past. Is being together what Ben would have wanted . . . or a betrayal of his memory that will eventually destroy them both?

About the Author

MOLLY McADAMS GREW up in California but now lives in the oh-so-amazing state of Texas with her husband, daughter, and fur babies. Her hobbies include hiking, snowboarding, traveling, and long walks on the beach . . . which roughly translates to being a homebody with her hubby and dishing out movie quotes.
www.mollysmcadams.com

Discover great authors, exclusive offers, and more at hc.com.

Give in to your impulses . . .
Read on for a sneak peek at six brand-new
e-book original tales of romance
from HarperCollins.
Available now wherever e-books are sold.

WHEN GOOD EARLS GO BAD
A Victorian Valentine's Day Novella
By Megan Frampton

THE WEDDING BAND
A Save the Date Novel
By Cara Connelly

RIOT
By Jamie Shaw

ONLY IN MY DREAMS
Ribbon Ridge Book One
By Darcy Burke

SINFUL REWARDS 1
A Billionaires and Bikers Novella
By Cynthia Sax

TEMPT THE NIGHT
A Trust No One Novel
By Dixie Lee Brown

An Excerpt from

WHEN GOOD EARLS GO BAD
A Victorian Valentine's Day Novella
by *Megan Frampton*

Megan Frampton's *Dukes Behaving Badly* series
continues, but this time it's an earl who's meeting
his match in a delightfully fun and sexy novella!

"While it's not precisely true that nobody is here, because I am, in fact, here, the truth is that there is no one here who can accommodate the request."

The man standing in the main area of the Quality Employment Agency didn't leave. She'd have to keep on, then.

"If I weren't here, then it would be even more in question, since you wouldn't know the answer to the question one way or the other, would you? So I am here, but I am not the proper person for what you need."

The man fidgeted with the hat he held in his hand. But still did not take her hint. She would have to persevere.

"I suggest you leave the information, and we will endeavor to fill the position when there is someone here who is not me." Annabelle gave a short nod of her head as she finished speaking, knowing she had been absolutely clear in what she'd said. If repetitive. So it was a surprise that the man to whom she was speaking was staring back at her, his mouth slightly opened, his eyes blinking behind his owlish spectacles. His hat now held very tightly in his hand.

Perhaps she should speak more slowly.

"We do not have a housekeeper for hire," she said, pausing

between each word. "I am the owner, not one of the employees for hire."

Now the man's mouth had closed, but it still seemed as though he did not understand.

"I do not understand," he said, confirming her very suspicion. "This is an employment agency, and I have an employer who wishes to find an employee. And if I do not find a suitable person within . . ." and at this he withdrew a pocket watch from his waistcoat and frowned at it, as though it was its fault it was already past tea time, and *goodness, wasn't she hungry and had Caroline left any milk in the jug? Because if not, well,* "twenty-four hours, my employer, the Earl of Selkirk, will be most displeased, and we will ensure your agency will no longer receive our patronage."

That last part drew her attention away from the issue of the milk and whether or not there was any.

"The Earl of . . . ?" she said, feeling that flutter in her stomach that signaled there was nobility present or being mentioned—or she wished there were, at least. Rather like the milk, actually.

"Selkirk," the man replied in a firm tone. He had no comment on the milk. And why would he? He didn't even know it was a possibility that they didn't have any, and if she did have to serve him tea, what would she say? Besides which, she had no clue to the man's name; he had just come in and been all brusque and demanded a housekeeper when there was none.

"Selkirk," Annabelle repeated, her mind rifling through all the nobles she'd ever heard mentioned.

"A Scottish earl," the man said.

Annabelle beamed and clapped her hands. "Oh, Scottish! Small wonder I did not recognize the title, I've only ever been in London and once to the seaside when I was five years old, but I wouldn't have known if that was Scotland, but I am fairly certain it was not because it would have been cold and it was quite warm in the water. Unless the weather was unseasonable, I can safely say I have never been to Scotland, nor do I know of any Scottish earls."

An Excerpt from

THE WEDDING BAND
A Save the Date Novel

by Cara Connelly

In the latest *Save the Date* novel from Cara
Connelly, journalist Christina Case crashes a
celebrity wedding, and sparks fly when she comes
face-to-face with A-list movie star Dakota Rain . . .

Dakota Rain took a good hard look in the bathroom mirror and inventoried the assets.

Piercing blue eyes? Check.

Sexy stubble? Check.

Sun-streaked blond hair? Check.

Movie-star smile?

Uh-oh.

In the doorway, his assistant rolled her eyes and hit speed dial. "Emily Fazzone here," she said. "Mr. Rain needs to see Dr. Spade this morning. Another cap." She listened a moment, then snorted a laugh. "You're telling me. Might as well cap them all and be done with it."

In the mirror Dakota gave her his hit man squint. "No extra caps."

"Weenie," she said, pocketing her phone. "You don't have time today, anyway. Spade's squeezing you in, as usual. Then you're due at the studio at eleven for the voice-over. It'll be tight, so step on it."

Deliberately, Dakota turned to his reflection again. Tilted his head. Pulled at his cheeks like he was contemplating a shave.

Emily did another eye roll. Muttering something that

might have been either "Get to work" or "What a jerk," she disappeared into his closet, emerging a minute later with jeans, T-shirt, and boxer briefs. She stacked them on the granite vanity, then pulled out her phone again and scrolled through the calendar.

"You've got a twelve o'clock with Peter at his office about the Levi's endorsement, then a one-thirty fitting for your tux. Mercer's coming here at two-thirty to talk about security for the wedding . . ."

Dakota tuned her out. His schedule didn't worry him. Emily would get him where he needed to be. If he ran a little late and a few people had to cool their heels, well, they were used to dealing with movie stars. Hell, they'd be disappointed if he behaved like regular folk.

Taking his sweet time, he shucked yesterday's briefs and meandered naked to the shower without thinking twice. He knew Emily wouldn't bat an eye. After ten years nursing him through injuries and illness, puking and pain, she'd seen all there was to see. Broad shoulders? Tight buns? She was immune.

And besides, she was gay.

Jacking the water temp to scalding, he stuck his head under the spray, wincing when it found the goose egg on the back of his skull. He measured it with his fingers, two inches around.

The same right hook that had chipped his tooth had bounced his head off a concrete wall.

Emily rapped on the glass. He rubbed a clear spot in the steam and gave her the hard eye for pestering him in the shower.

She was immune to that too. "I asked you if we're looking at a lawsuit."

"Damn straight." He was all indignation. "We're suing The Combat Zone. Tubby busted my tooth and gave me a concussion to boot."

She sighed. "I meant, are *we* getting sued? Tubby's a good bouncer. If he popped you, you gave him a reason."

Dakota put a world of aggrievement into his Western drawl. "Why do you always take everybody else's side? You weren't there. You don't know what happened."

"Sure I do. It's October, isn't it? The month you start howling at the moon and throwing punches at bystanders. It's an annual event. The lawyers are on standby. I just want to know if I should call them."

He did the snarl that sent villains and virgins running for their mamas.

An Excerpt from

RIOT

by *Jamie Shaw*

Jamie Shaw's rock stars are back, and this time wild, unpredictable Dee and sexy, mohawked guitarist Joel have explosive chemistry—but will jealousy and painful memories keep them apart?

"Kiss me," I order the luckiest guy in Mayhem tonight. When he sat next to me at the bar earlier with his "Leave It to Beaver" haircut, I made sure to avoid eye contact and cross my legs in the opposite direction. I didn't think I'd end up making out with him, but now I have no choice.

A dumb expression washes over his face. He might be cute if he didn't look so. freaking. dumb. "Huh?"

"Oh for God's sake."

I curl my fingers behind his neck and yank him to my mouth, tilting my head to the side and hoping he's a quick learner. My lips part, my tongue comes out to play, and after a moment, he finally catches on. His greedy fingers bury themselves in my chocolate brown curls—which I spent *hours* on this morning.

Peeking out of the corner of my eye, I spot Joel Gibbon stroll past me, a bleach-blonde groupie tucked under his arm. He's too busy whispering in her ear to notice me, and my fingers itch to punch him in the back of his stupid mohawked head to get his attention.

I'm preparing to push Leave It to Beaver off me when Joel's gaze finally lifts to meet mine. I bite Beaver's bottom lip between my teeth and give it a little tug, and the corner of

Joel's mouth lifts up into an infuriating smirk that is *so* not the reaction I wanted. He continues walking, and when he's finally out of sight, I break my lips from Beaver's and nudge him back toward his own stool, immediately spinning in the opposite direction to scowl at my giggling best friend.

"I can't BELIEVE him!" I shout at a far-too-amused-looking Rowan. How does she not recognize the gravity of this situation?!

I'm about to shake some sense into her when Beaver taps me on the shoulder. "Um—"

"You're welcome," I say with a flick of my wrist, not wanting to waste another minute on a guy who can't appreciate how long it took me to get my hair to curl like this—or at least make messing it up worth my while.

Rowan gives him an apologetic half smile, and I let out a deep sigh.

I don't feel bad about Beaver. I feel bad about the dickhead bass guitarist for the Last Ones to Know.

"That boy is making me insane," I growl.

Rowan turns a bright smile on me, her blue eyes sparkling with humor. "You were already insane."

"He's making me homicidal," I clarify, and she laughs.

"Why don't you just tell him you like him?" She twirls two tiny straws in her cocktail, her eyes periodically flitting up to the stage. She's waiting for Adam, and I'd probably be jealous of her if those two weren't so disgustingly perfect for each other.

Last semester, I nearly got kicked out of my dorm when I let Rowan move in with me and my roommate. But Rowan's asshole live-in boyfriend had cheated on her, and she had nowhere to go, and she's been my *best* friend since kindergarten. I ignored the written warnings from my RA, and Rowan ultimately ended up moving in with Adam before I got kicked out. Fast forward to one too many "overnight visitors" later, I still ended up getting reported, and Rowan and I got a two-bedroom in an apartment complex near campus. Her name is on the lease right next to mine, but really, the apartment is just a decoy she uses to avoid telling her parents that she's actually living with three ungodly hot rock stars. She sleeps in Adam's bed, his bandmate Shawn is in the second bedroom, and Joel sleeps on their couch most nights because he's a hot, stupid, infuriating freaking nomad.

"Because I *don't* like him," I answer. When I realize my drink is gone, I steal Rowan's, down the last of it, and flag the bartender.

"Then why is he making you insane?"

"Because *he* doesn't like *me*."

Rowan lifts a sandy blonde eyebrow at me, but I don't expect her to understand. Hell, *I* don't understand. I've never wanted a boy to like me so badly in my entire life.

An Excerpt from

ONLY IN MY DREAMS
Ribbon Ridge Book One
by Darcy Burke

From a *USA Today* bestselling author
comes the first installment in a sexy and
emotional family saga about seven siblings
who reunite in a small Oregon town to
fulfill their brother's dying wish . . .

Sara Archer took a deep breath and dialed her assistant and close friend, Craig Walker. He was going to laugh his butt off when she told him why she was calling, which almost made her hang up, but she forced herself to go through with it.

"Sara! Your call can only mean one thing: you're totally doing it."

She envisioned his blue eyes alight with laughter, his dimples creasing, and rolled her eyes. "I guess so."

He whooped into the phone, causing Sara to pull it back from her ear. "Awesome! You won't regret it. It's been waaaaay too long since you got out there. What, four years?"

"You're exaggerating." More like three. She hadn't been out with a guy since Jude. Easy, breezy, coffee barista Jude. He'd been a welcome breath of fresh air after her cheating college boyfriend. Come to think of it, she'd taken three years to get back in the game then too.

"Am I? I've known you for almost three years, and you've never had even a casual date in all that time."

Because after she and Jude had ended their fling, she'd decided to focus on her business, and she'd hired Craig a couple of months later. "Enough with the history lesson. Let's talk about tonight before I lose my nerve."

"Got it. I'm really proud of you for doing this. You need a social life beyond our rom-com movie nights."

Sara suspected he was pushing her to go out because he'd started dating someone. They seemed serious even though it had been only a couple of weeks, and when you fell in love, you wanted the whole world to fall in love too. Not that Sara planned on doing that again—if she could even count her college boyfriend as falling in love. She really didn't know anymore.

"I was thinking I might go line dancing." She glanced through her clothing, pondering what to wear.

"Line dancing?" Craig's tone made it sound as if he were asking whether she was going to the garbage dump. He wouldn't have been caught dead in a country-western bar. "If you want to get your groove on, Taylor and I will come get you and take you downtown. Much better scene."

No, the nearby suburban country-western bar would suit her needs just fine. She wouldn't be comfortable at a chic Portland club—totally out of her league. "I'll stick with Sidewinders, thanks."

"We wouldn't take you to a gay bar," Craig said with a touch of exasperation that made her smile.

"I know. I just don't want company. You'd try to set me up with every guy in the place."

"I'm not that bad! Taylor keeps me in line."

Yeah, she'd noticed. She'd been out with them once and was surprised at the difference in Craig. He was still his energetic self, but it was like everything he had was focused on his new boyfriend. She supposed that was natural when a relationship was shiny and new. "Well, I'm good going by myself. I'm just going to dance a little, maybe sip a lemon drop, see what happens."

Craig made a noise of disgust. "Don't ass out, Sara. You need to get laid."

An Excerpt from

SINFUL REWARDS 1
A Billionaires and Bikers Novella
by Cynthia Sax

Belinda "Bee" Carter is a good girl; at least, that's
what she tells herself. And a good girl deserves
a nice guy—just like the gorgeous and moody
billionaire Nicolas Rainer. Or so she thinks,
until she takes a look through her telescope
and sees a naked, tattooed man on the balcony
across the courtyard. He has been watching
her, and that makes him all the more enticing.
But when a mysterious and anonymous text
message dares her to do something bad, she
must decide if she is really the good girl she has
always claimed to be, or if she's willing to risk
everything for her secret fantasy of being watched.

An Avon Red Impulse Novella

I'd told Cyndi I'd never use it, that it was an instrument purchased by perverts to spy on their neighbors. She'd laughed and called me a prude, not knowing that I was one of those perverts, that I secretly yearned to watch and be watched, to care and be cared for.

If I'm cautious, and I'm always cautious, she'll never realize I used her telescope this morning. I swing the tube toward the bench and adjust the knob, bringing the mysterious object into focus.

It's a phone. Nicolas's phone. I bounce on the balls of my feet. This is a sign, another declaration from fate that we belong together. I'll return Nicolas's much-needed device to him. As a thank you, he'll invite me to dinner. We'll talk. He'll realize how perfect I am for him, fall in love with me, marry me.

Cyndi will find a fiancé also—everyone loves her—and we'll have a double wedding, as sisters of the heart often do. It'll be the first wedding my family has had in generations.

Everyone will watch us as we walk down the aisle. I'll wear a strapless white Vera Wang mermaid gown with organza and lace details, crystal and pearl embroidery accents, the bodice fitted, and the skirt hemmed for my shorter height. My hair will be swept up. My shoes—

Voices murmur outside the condo's door, the sound piercing my delightful daydream. I swing the telescope upward, not wanting to be caught using it. The snippets of conversation drift away.

I don't relax. If the telescope isn't positioned in the same way as it was last night, Cyndi will realize I've been using it. She'll tease me about being a fellow pervert, sharing the story, embellished for dramatic effect, with her stern, serious dad—or, worse, with Angel, that snobby friend of hers.

I'll die. It'll be worse than being the butt of jokes in high school because that ridicule was about my clothes and this will center on the part of my soul I've always kept hidden. It'll also be the truth, and I won't be able to deny it. I am a pervert.

I have to return the telescope to its original position. This is the only acceptable solution. I tap the metal tube.

Last night, my man-crazy roommate was giggling over the new guy in three-eleven north. The previous occupant was a gray-haired, bowtie-wearing tax auditor, his luxurious accommodations supplied by Nicolas. The most exciting thing he ever did was drink his tea on the balcony.

According to Cyndi, the new occupant is a delicious piece of man candy—tattooed, buff, and head-to-toe lickable. He was completing armcurls outside, and she enthusiastically counted his reps, oohing and aahing over his bulging biceps, calling to me to take a look.

I resisted that temptation, focusing on making macaroni and cheese for the two of us, the recipe snagged from the diner my mom works in. After we scarfed down dinner, Cyndi licking her plate clean, she left for the club and hasn't returned.

Three-eleven north is the mirror condo to ours. I straighten the telescope. That position looks about right, but then, the imitation UGGs I bought in my second year of college looked about right also. The first time I wore the boots in the rain, the sheepskin fell apart, leaving me barefoot in Economics 201.

Unwilling to risk Cyndi's friendship on "about right," I gaze through the eyepiece. The view consists of rippling golden planes, almost like . . .

Tanned skin pulled over defined abs.

I blink. It can't be. I take another look. A perfect pearl of perspiration clings to a puckered scar. The drop elongates more and more, stretching, snapping. It trickles downward, navigating the swells and valleys of a man's honed torso.

No. I straighten. This is wrong. I shouldn't watch our sexy neighbor as he stands on his balcony. If anyone catches me . . .

Parts 1 – 8 available now!

An Excerpt from

TEMPT THE NIGHT
A Save the Date Novel

by Dixie Lee Brown

Dixie Lee Brown concludes her thrilling
Trust No One series with the fast-paced
tale of a damaged hero and the sexy
fugitive he can't help falling for.

She pursed her lips and studied him. "That's deep, Brady." A crooked grin gradually appeared, erasing the worry wrinkles from her forehead. Then, without any encouragement from him, Mac took a step closer and leaned into his chest, sliding her arms around his waist.

He hesitated only a second before wrapping her in his arms and pulling her close. A groan escaped him.

She shifted her head to glance up. "Do you mind?"

A soft chuckle vibrated through him. "Sugar, I'll hold you anytime, anywhere."

Mac snuggled closer, and he tipped her head with his fingers, slowly covering her mouth with his, giving her plenty of time to change her mind. When she didn't, he drank of her sweetness like a man dying of thirst. Again and again he kissed her, his tongue pushing into her mouth, swirling and dancing with hers. He couldn't get enough of her full, soft lips, her sweet taste, and the bold way she pressed against him.

Brady couldn't say which of the day's events was responsible for her change in temperature where he was concerned, but it wasn't important. They were taking steps in the right direction, and he wasn't going to do anything to screw that up. He wanted her warm and willing in his hands, but he also wanted her there for the right reasons. The decision was hers to make.

When he lifted his head, there were tears on her eyelashes, but her smile made his heart grab an extra beat. He let his fingers trail across the satin skin of her cheek as he kissed her neck tenderly and breathed in her sweet scent.

"God, you smell good." He kissed each of her closed eyes, then leaned his forehead on hers and took a deep breath. "I'd love for this to go on all night. Unfortunately, Joe wants us to meet with Maria." He steadied her as she straightened and took a step back.

Mac's gaze was uncertain. "We could meet later . . . if you want to . . ."

"Aw, sugar. If *I* want to? That's like asking if I want to keep breathing." He threaded his fingers through her hair and brushed his lips over hers. "I've wanted you since the first time you lied to me." Brady chuckled as her eyes lit up.

She punched his chest with a fisted hand. "Hey! That was the only time I lied, and I had a darn good reason. Some big galoot knocks me down, pounces on me, and then expects me to be truthful. Nuh uh. I don't think so." Her eyes sparkled with challenge.

"*Galoot*, huh? No more John Wayne movies for you, sugar."

She sucked in a big breath, and he could tell by the mischief in her eyes that she was getting ready to let him have it. He touched his fingers to her lips to silence her. "Let me say this, okay? There's a good chance we'll go in and meet with Maria, and sometime before, after, or during, you'll think about us—about me—and decide we're not a good idea. I want you to know two things. First . . . it's the best idea I've had in a long time. Second . . . if you decide it's a mistake or that you're not ready to get any closer, that's okay. No pressure."

He stepped back and gave her some room. It struck him that he'd just lied to her. What he said would have been true for any other woman he'd ever known, but he damn sure wasn't going to give up on Mac that easily.

A grin made the sparkle in her eyes dance as she slipped her hand into his. "Obviously you're confusing me with some other woman, because I don't usually change my mind once it's made up, and I'm a big girl, so you can stop worrying that your charm, good looks, and sex appeal will bowl me over. As for thinking about you—yeah." She stepped closer and lowered her voice to a silky whisper. "You might cross my mind once or twice . . . so let's get this meeting over with."

"You got it, sugar." Brady couldn't remember when he'd been so contented—or when he'd ever used that word to describe himself before. Whether or not tonight ended with him in bed with this amazingly beautiful and brave woman didn't really matter. The last few minutes had made it clear that his interest in her went way beyond just the prospect of sex. He wanted everything she had to give. *Shit!* She'd turned him upside down and inside out until he doubted his own ability to walk away . . . or even if he wanted to.